The Secret Baby
Day Leclaire

Harlequin Books

TORONTO • NEW YORK • LONDON
AMSTERDAM • PARIS • SYDNEY • HAMBURG
STOCKHOLM • ATHENS • TOKYO • MILAN
MADRID • WARSAW • BUDAPEST • AUCKLAND

To my mom, Hazen F. Totton, and my sister,
Diane H. Andre, for all their love, encouragement and
endless patience. Thank you. You two are incredible!

ISBN 0-373-03457-1

THE SECRET BABY

First North American Publication 1997.

Copyright © 1995 by Day Totton Smith.

This edition published by arrangement with Harlequin Books S.A.

® and TM are trademarks of the publisher. Trademarks indicated with
® are registered in the United States Patent and Trademark Office, the
Canadian Trade Marks Office and in other countries.

Printed in U.S.A.

PROLOGUE

HE'D done it. He had her. And soon…very soon…Sable Jameson Caldwell would know it.

Damien Hawke dropped into the over-stuffed white chair behind the huge, pretentious desk, a tight, grim smile playing about his mouth. The contract, signed and executed, lay before him on the white marble tabletop. He wouldn't have been human if he hadn't savored his moment of triumph. Savored the knowledge that after five long years he had Sable at his mercy. But it wasn't enough, he acknowledged. He didn't want her construction business—or, rather, her late husband's construction business. He wanted her.

And this time she wouldn't escape.

A small sound from the far side of the white and crimson office caught Damien's attention and he lifted his head. 'Have the arrangements been made, Lute?' he asked.

In response to the question, a huge man slipped silently from the shadows, his bald head gleaming in the subdued light. In years past, Lute's position would have been called many things. Valet, manservant, gentleman's gentleman. Damien simply called him friend.

'The movers will be here tonight to strip the room and deliver the furnishings to Miss Patricia.'

'Excellent.'

Damien stood and strode around the pedestaled desk, his shoes sinking into the blood-red carpeting. A large leopardskin floor covering blocked his path and with the toe of his shoe he kicked the pelt to one side. His gaze shifted over the exotic animal heads mounted on the harsh white walls and a flicker of distaste touched his stern features at the blatant obscenity. Every one of them was on the endangered species list.

'She will want her dead animals returned, yes?' Lute questioned.

'Knowing Patricia, I don't doubt it for a minute.'

Lute sighed. 'She dishonors her brother's memory and betrays her sister-in-law by selling her share of the family business but keeps her gaudy bits and pieces. Strange woman.'

Damien shrugged negligently. He couldn't care less about Patricia Caldwell. Not anymore. She'd served her purpose by giving him what he wanted most—forty percent of Caldwell's stock. It was the same percentage as Sable controlled. 'Money is Patricia's god. It always has been.'

Blackness settled on Lute's face. He smoothed his thumb and index finger across his white moustache and down to the narrow beard that framed his chin. It was a familiar gesture, a gesture that betrayed an inner turmoil. Damien folded his arms across his chest and waited for his friend to speak his piece.

'Money is a demanding god. A deadly god,' Lute said, before adding softly, 'But then, so is revenge.'

Damien's mouth tightened. He hadn't chosen the path he walked blindly. He'd taken every step with great deliberation. 'I want this room sanitized.' He spoke harshly, but Lute didn't flinch. Only one other person could confront Damien's anger with equanimity, with a soothing touch that calmed even the most savage beast. And he rarely spoke her name. 'I don't want one trace of cigarette smoke or that cloying perfume Patricia drenches herself in to remain.'

Lute inclined his head. 'It will be done. By Monday morning the office will be yours.' He turned to go.

'Have you seen her, Lute?' The question was torn from Damien, unexpected and unwelcome. They both knew of whom he spoke.

Sable.

'Yes.' The acknowledgement sounded hesitant, regretful. 'I have seen her.'

Damien tensed. 'And?'

'She looks much the same. Thinner, perhaps.'

'That's all?'

Lute turned around, his reluctance unmistakable. 'There were... shadows. Much sadness,' he admitted. His snowy brows drew together over soft blue eyes—eyes as old as time and as guileless as a baby's. 'And more sadness to come, yes?'

Again Damien shrugged. 'That's up to her. If she sells her shares of Caldwell's to me as Patricia did, she can walk away a wealthy woman. If she chooses to fight me...' his odd green eyes glittered with ruthless intent '...then I'll break her.'

'She will fight you,' Lute said, and without another word he left the room.

Damien stood motionless for a moment, his thoughtful gaze settling on the door that connected this office—*his* office—with the adjoining one. He didn't hesitate. He crossed to the door. The handle turned easily beneath his hand, the heavy oak panel swinging silently open. A single light, probably left on by the cleaning crew, shone from the desk by the windows. He walked into the room, leaving behind the hellish opulence that so suited Patricia for a soothing warmth guaranteed to assuage even the most tortured soul—stepping from harsh gold and crimson excess to the soft, mellow rose and yellow of Eden's garden.

Moonlight filtered through the tinted floor-to-ceiling windows, gilding the room with silver, and he shut the connecting door, shutting out the stink of stale tobacco and musk. The air here was sweet and smelled of Sable. He inhaled deeply, dragging the clean, fresh scent of her into his lungs.

And he remembered... Remembered their time together, their passion, their desperate need, their oneness. And her betrayal... He remembered that most of all.

For it wasn't a betrayal he'd easily forget... or forgive—a fact Sable would soon learn.

CHAPTER ONE

SABLE sensed him long before she saw him. She didn't need to turn around and search the crowd of faces behind her. The elevator was too packed to allow it, anyway. But she knew he was there. Somewhere.

She could feel the heavy touch of his gaze stroking along her spine as surely as if he'd reached out and put his hands on her. She closed her eyes, fighting her instinctive reaction. It had been so long since she'd felt the insidious yearning only he could arouse, felt the subtle clenching of inner muscles that signaled his presence. Her hand tightened on her briefcase and her breathing grew shallow. How could she still feel this way after five long, lonely years?

The elevator stopped and the doors parted, releasing a small wave of people, before drawing more in, pushing her deeper into the car and closer to...him. She shifted to one side and risked turning her head a fraction, allowing her gaze to drift casually over the occupants behind her. She stiffened. A man with distinctively streaked tawny hair stood with his shoulder braced against the back wall. Her heart pounded and acute fear momentarily robbed her of all thought, leaving behind blind panic—and a desperate, instinctive need to escape. Only the press of people held her in place.

Dear lord. It *was* him.

Her nails bit into her palm, the pain sharp and cruel. She barely noticed. All her attention was focused on him—and on what his return might mean. She drew in a shaky breath, forcing herself to suppress an almost overwhelming emotional response and to think. *Think*, damn it! she silently ordered. Why had he come? He'd only bring more misery. Misery and danger—danger should he discover all she'd kept hidden from him these past five years.

She faced forward. He didn't move—the distorted reflection from the copper-tinted doors told her that much. Instead he continued to lounge against the rear wall, waiting... waiting for what? For the car finally to be empty? For them finally to be alone? If she got off at an earlier floor, would he follow? She knew the answer to that. If she got off, he would too. And he'd know she'd panicked because of him. She didn't dare give him that much of an edge. Still... The pivotal question remained, scraping across sensitive nerve-endings like a serrated blade.

What did he want?

The next stop brought another influx of passengers and to her horror she found herself forced farther and farther back until she stood just in front of him.

'Sable,' he said in a husky undertone, the sound of his voice stirring fragments of bittersweet memories. When she didn't respond, he placed his hand on the small of her back. His fingers slipped over the soft rose silk of her skirt, closing on the narrow curve of her hip. He tugged her against him. 'Or should I say—Mrs Caldwell?'

She couldn't pull loose—they were packed in too tightly. 'Stop it!' she ordered, keeping her voice whisper-soft. She shot a quick glance to either side, relieved beyond measure to discover that the people nearest to them were caught up in their own quiet discussions. No one was paying the least attention to her.

Floor by floor the elevator progressed relentlessly upward. The moment a space opened in front of her, she tried to step forward, but he stopped her. He tightened his hold, pulling her deeper into his embrace, the warmth of his body cutting through the silk of her suit. His hand shifted to her waist, his fingers sliding beneath the bottom of her jacket and splaying across her abdomen, moving in an insidious caress. 'Not yet, my love. I'm enjoying this too much,' he murmured, his breath stirring the curls at her temple.

She stifled her cry of alarm, not daring to say anything, not daring to draw attention to her predicament. Instead she forced herself to be perfectly still and wait as the elevator dispersed passenger after passenger, moving ever upward toward her office on the executive floor. She felt like a mouse trapped in a cage with a ravenous tomcat—and nowhere to escape. Claustrophobia mounted with each stop they made, with every breath she drew. His soft laughter rumbled in her ear and she knew he found her helplessness amusing.

The car eased to a halt once more and the final occupant departed. It seemed to take an eternity before the doors slid closed, sequestering them in the small metal cubicle. Not waiting another moment, Sable ripped free of his hold. Then, gathering every bit of strength, feeling more vulnerable than she had in a long, long time, she turned and faced him.

Damien Hawke. Her former employer, former lover…and the father of her four-year-old son. Was that why he'd come? Had he somehow found out about Kyle? His expression gave nothing away. But then, it never did.

She forced herself to look up at him and instantly regretted it. She'd forgotten how intense his eyes could be. Or perhaps she'd chosen to forget. She could lose her very soul in those odd green eyes. They glowed with an inner light, hard and knowing and compelling, mesmerizing her in a way that was all to frighteningly familiar. They were the pale green of an arctic wasteland—fiery emotion encased in impenetrable ice. She'd never yet read an article about him that failed to mention the disconcerting power of those eyes.

'Hello, Damien,' she managed to say in an even voice. 'You always did have the most objectionable ways of making your presence known.'

He inclined his head, his gaze mocking. 'You're too kind.'

'Touching me like that... It was rude. It was...' She glared at him. 'It was unconscionable.'

He shrugged. 'It felt good. You know it did.'

She turned slightly, stung by the bitter truth, hoping she was managing to hide the intense, piercing desire, the gnawing hunger that being near him stirred. How could she have been so foolish as to believe those emotions had died? She took a deep, calming breath, drawing on all her professional reserves to see her through this unexpected confrontation.

'What are you doing here?' she asked with a composure that threatened to desert her at any moment. 'It can't be coincidental. It never is with you.'

He tilted his head to one side, watching her with open amusement. He possessed a disconcerting stillness, like a jungle cat—lazy, graceful and ready to pounce at the slightest provocation. 'You know me that well?'

'I know you all *too* well,' she responded tautly. 'I repeat, what are you doing here?'

He shrugged, a simple, careless movement. But she'd learned from long, hard experience that nothing Damien did was simple. And his actions were never, ever careless. 'I warned you I'd be back,' he said.

'No,' she corrected him, daring to meet his gaze once more. 'You warned you'd have your revenge.'

His amusement died, leaving behind a wintry resolve she couldn't mistake. 'So I did. Thanks for the reminder.'

She fought to conceal her apprehension, knowing he'd be quick to take advantage if he sensed her vulnerability. When she'd worked with him, she'd admired his hunter's instinct, admired how that instinct had never once failed him. Now she feared it. 'Is that why you've returned? To take your revenge?'

'And if I have?'

The elevator eased to a stop and the doors opened. She hesitated, part of her desperate to leave the confines of the car and escape his presence. But another, more rational part warned that she'd be wise to find out what he wanted. He stepped forward, bracing open the doors, standing so close that she could once again feel the heat of his body, smell his spicy, distinctive cologne.

She searched his face, hoping for a clue to his thoughts. He wasn't a handsome man in the classic sense of the word; his features were far too strong, too potently masculine. But the high, arching cheekbones, the full, sensual mouth and knowing look in his eyes drew women with effortless ease. He was like a huge, lazy lion, powerful and secure in his domain. And he had no intention of revealing anything until he was good and ready.

He returned her gaze with an implacable reserve, forcing Sable to ask once again, 'Will you tell me why you're here?'

'Yes... In time.'

With a small exclamation of frustration, she started from the car. He reached out just as she passed, his fingers brushing her cheek. 'Still like silk,' he murmured.

She pulled back sharply, stepping into the hallway outside the elevator. 'Don't do that!' She hated the mocking humor that lit his eyes, the way he shook his head in mild reproof.

'That isn't what you used to say,' he murmured. 'You used to beg for my touch.'

She stared at him in disbelief, her black eyes huge and wounded. Cruelty had never been part of his nature. But then, she didn't know this Damien. Not anymore. Gathering the shreds of her dignity, she lifted her chin. Well, he didn't know her either. Five years had changed them both.

'Thank you for the reminder,' she said with gentle irony. 'I've made a point of learning from my past mistakes since we parted.'

'As have I.' His voice dropped, but she heard every harsh word as though he'd shouted. 'And you were a big mistake, weren't you, Sable? I'd have been better off embracing an adder. But the time's come to correct past errors.'

'Meaning?' she demanded.

'Meaning that you're going down. And I'm going to drag you there every hellish step of the way.'

That said, he stepped back into the car, leaving her to stare in shocked disbelief as the doors silently closed between them. How long she stood there she didn't know. It wasn't until her secretary touched her arm that she awoke to her surroundings.

'Mrs Caldwell? Are you all right?' Janine asked in concern.

Sable blinked. 'I'm sorry?'

'You're so pale. And look—you've dropped your briefcase.'

Glancing down in confusion, Sable saw that the black case had slipped from her numb fingers and lay drunkenly on its side. 'Thank you, Janine,' she murmured, stooping to pick up the briefcase. 'I'm fine.'

'Are you sure?' her secretary persisted. 'You don't look fine. You look rather...ill.'

Sable sighed. Janine had been her husband Leonard's secretary. After his death, she'd been offered a promotion, but insisted she'd be of more service working with Sable, helping in her struggle to gain control of the business and solve the problems of a company on the skids. And though Janine never unbent sufficiently to use Sable's first name she took a proprietorial interest in all aspects of Caldwell's, including her employer's well-being.

'Thank you, but I'm all right now,' Sable said, a hint of reserve coloring her tone. As much as she appreciated Janine's concern, she wasn't in the mood to field the older woman's questions. 'Do you have my notes prepared for the board meeting?' she asked, steering the conversation into safer channels.

Janine's mouth tightened, but she didn't press the issue. 'Yes, Mrs Caldwell. They're on your desk.'

Sable forced her mind to business matters, grateful for the need to concentrate, for the need to push every other consideration to the back of her mind. 'There should be a tape full of correspondence on the Dictaphone for you to transcribe. I'd like the letters to go out today. Is Patricia in yet?' At the lack of an immediate response, Sable raised an eyebrow in question. 'Janine?'

'Why, no, Mrs Caldwell. She isn't.'

That was a surprise. For all Patricia's faults, her sister-in-law always arrived early to work. 'Is it possible she's forgotten the board meeting is today?'

'I very much doubt it,' her secretary replied. 'I reminded her of it myself. Will there be anything else?'

'Nothing for now, thank you. Start on those letters if you will,' Sable replied, opening the door to her office. 'I'd like to review my notes before the meeting, so hold all my calls, please.'

'Even if it's Miss Trainer?'

Sable turned, a small frown creasing her brow. 'My request never includes her. You know that.' It was an inviolate rule that Kyle's nanny could interrupt any time, any place. Why would Janine think that had changed?

The secretary gave a small shrug. 'My mistake.'

'That's all right.' More than anything Sable wanted to escape into her office before the last vestiges of her strength ebbed completely away. Instead, she forced herself to stand patiently and offer an encouraging smile. After all, Janine was a valued employee. She shouldn't take the fallout for Damien's actions. 'I appreciate your checking. Is there anything else you need to discuss with me?'

'No. I'll get right to work on those letters.'

'I'd appreciate it.'

With a sigh of relief, Sable shut the door between her office and the reception area. Leaning against the sturdy oak panel, her head drooped like a flower on a broken stem. Here it was, only eight-thirty in the morning, and already exhaustion gripped her. Still ahead lay the board meeting—always a stressful occasion—not to mention discovering the purpose behind Damien's visit.

She glanced across the room toward Patricia's office. The door that separated them remained shut, not even the acrid stench of cigarette smoke seeping past the sturdy barrier. That in itself was unusual enough, a convincing testimony to Patricia's absence. Had she decided to boycott the meeting? It was a distinct possibility. Her sister-in-law hadn't taken kindly to being stripped of the chairmanship last month. If she could find a way to cause trouble, she'd do it.

With a sigh, Sable straightened and headed for the private bathroom that adjoined her office. Once there, she stared in the mirror over the sink for a long moment. Janine was right. She did look ill. All color had fled her face, leaving her cheeks ashen, her pallor intensified by the cloud of unruly black curls that had escaped the formal knot at the nape of her neck. Worst of all, her dark eyes were like two huge, bruised smudges, betraying all too clearly her vulnerability.

If Damien had seen her like this, he'd be after her like a shark on a blood trail. And he'd be just as brutal and merciless. Not wasting another minute, she opened a drawer in the built-in vanity and removed a cosmetics case. Applying blush and shadow with a practiced hand, she managed to conceal most of the outer traces of her distress. A final touch of rose-toned lipstick added the perfect amount of color to her face.

Turning her attention to her hair, she pulled out the pins that anchored it in place. Heavy curls fell in an unruly mass past her shoulders, effectively destroying the image of the super-competent executive. But not for long. A bit of water and a brisk brushing helped tame the more stubborn strands and she swiftly rolled her hair into a tight, formal knot.

Sparing a swift glance at her watch, she groaned in dismay. She had precisely twenty minutes to get organized. Hurrying to her desk, she sat down and flipped open the file Janine had prepared. But no matter how hard she tried to focus on her notes she couldn't stop her treacherous thoughts from centering on Damien and how his return would change her life.

Turning her chair to face the window, she stared out at the San Francisco skyline. Why had he come back? Why now, after all this time? She closed her eyes, rubbing a weary hand across her brow. She had a thousand questions—questions to which only Damien had the answers. And, knowing him, she wouldn't like those answers one little bit.

The moments before the start of the board meeting seemed like some horrible replay of her experience that morning in the elevator. Sable stood at the buffet with her back to the conference room, pouring a cup of coffee from a heavy silver carafe. The sudden thread of alarm that snaked along her spine caught her completely by surprise. Once again she felt the ominous clenching of her muscles, the swift, uncontrollable touch of desire bringing all her senses to full flower. And in that instant she knew *he* had returned.

Cornelius Becker, the board's oldest member, approached. 'Who is it that just walked in?' he demanded querulously. 'That man over there by the door. Doesn't he know executive sessions are closed to general members?'

Giving herself time to school her features into a composed mask, she returned the carafe to the table and added cream to her coffee. She turned slowly, certain of whom she'd see. Sure enough, standing in comfortable solitude, his mantle of authority absolute, was Damien. His gaze met hers from across the room, his brilliant green eyes alive with passionate secrets.

'That's Damien Hawke,' she said quietly, and took a quick, restorative sip of coffee.

'*The* Damien Hawke?' Cornelius sounded impressed. 'Do you know him?'

'Yes,' she admitted, her response sounding short to the point of rudeness. To her relief, Cornelius didn't appear to notice.

'I've wanted to meet him for quite some time now. Hawke is a brilliant businessman, positively brilliant.' He chuckled, his eyes inquisitive beneath his bushy brows. 'But then, if you know him, you're already aware of that, aren't you?'

'Yes,' she said, hoping the reluctance in her voice wasn't too apparent. 'I am.'

'Introduce me, my dear.' He rubbed his hands together in anticipation. 'I'm curious to know why he's here.'

A dozen excuses leapt to her lips, but she didn't voice a single one. Instead she returned her cup and saucer to the buffet table and walked with Cornelius across the room. He'd been her chief advocate when Patricia had fought to oust her from the board after Leonard's death a year ago. Without his backing, Sable would have lost everything. He'd also been the one to recommend her for the chairmanship in Patricia's stead when their business situation had worsened. His request was a small price to pay. Besides, she could handle a simple introduction, couldn't she?

She stopped directly in front of Damien, aware of the challenge in his eyes. Did he think he could cow her with one of his infamous looks of intimidation? He had a lot to learn. 'Cornelius, I'd like to introduce you to Damien Hawke. Damien, this is Cornelius Becker, one of our senior board members.'

The two men shook hands. 'I'm surprised to see Caldwell's biggest competitor at our board meeting,' Cornelius said. 'Do you own stock in Caldwell's?'

Damien folded his arms across his chest. 'Yes. I do.'

Sable couldn't conceal her shock. Her gaze flashed to Damien's. 'A recent acquisition?' she asked, amazed that her voice came out as steady as it did.

'Very recent,' he confirmed.

'You are aware that this is an executive session of the board?' Cornelius questioned. 'I'm afraid it's closed to common shareholders.'

'But then, I'm not a common shareholder,' Damien stated gently. 'And if there are no objections I'd like to address the board before the meeting.'

Cornelius frowned. 'Your request is highly unusual,' he observed. 'The decision will have to be Sable's.'

Damien's expression didn't change. He glanced at her. 'Do you have any objection?'

He wasn't surprised that the final decision would be hers, she realized. Which meant he'd known all along that she was the chairwoman. And in that instant true fear gripped her. Nothing that had happened so far today had been an accident. He had a purpose in coming. If she hadn't been so thrown by the shock of seeing him in the elevator, she'd have figured that out sooner. He'd wanted her off-balance because it gave him the advantage.

The question still remained, though... Her distraction gave him the advantage to do *what*?

'What are you up to, Damien?' she demanded. 'You never do anything without a game plan.' She'd learned that crucial lesson during the four years she'd worked for him. And, more often than not, by the time his competitor realized what that game plan might be, it was far too late. Apprehension gripped her. Could that be the case this time? Was she too late to alter his scheme?

A lazy smile tugged at his mouth. 'Finally catching on?' he asked. 'You never used to be so slow. Or perhaps you've just grown complacent. Not wise in today's business world.' His smile died. 'Not wise at all when you have competitors waiting to pounce on your most insignificant error.'

There was no mistaking the threat. It took every scrap of composure to turn to Cornelius and force out a light laugh. 'I've been rude to our guest. I've neglected to offer Mr Hawke some coffee. I don't suppose...?'

'Allow me, my dear,' Cornelius suggested with alacrity. 'How do you take it, Mr Hawke?'

'Make it Damien,' he replied. 'And I prefer my coffee like most things in life.' His gaze locked with Sable's, his words directed at her every bit as much as at Cornelius. 'Straight up and uncorrupted.'

'Black it is,' Cornelius said with a chuckle. 'And why don't I bring you another cup, Sable? Half coffee and half cream, right?'

'That's very kind of you,' she murmured.

'My pleasure,' he replied, and crossed the room to join the other board members milling around the buffet table.

'You're as charming as always,' Damien said the instant the older man had moved out of earshot. 'But then, that's your specialty, isn't it?'

'What is? Charm?' she asked, lifting an eyebrow in question.

'Charming old men, to be precise.'

She sucked in her breath, hot color blossoming across her cheekbones. 'How dare you?' she whispered.

He released a short, dry laugh. 'Why act so insulted? Your charm was a talent you used while working for me. A talent you used to hook a husband old enough to be your father. And a talent you continue to use, if Cornelius Becker's reaction is the norm.'

She refused to dignify his comment with a response. There wasn't any point. He'd think what he chose, no matter what she said. 'What's going on?' she questioned instead. 'What do you want, Damien?'

He tilted his head to one side. 'Wasn't my request clear enough for you? I want to address the board.'

Her hands balled into fists. 'That's not what I'm referring to and you know it. It's been five years. If you're here, it's to cause trouble. Why now, after all this time?'

He leaned closer, his voice low and intimate. 'Some things take time. Depending on what they are, it can even be worth the wait.' His eyes darkened, the intense green as cold and turbulent as a mountain stream. 'Especially when it comes to revenge.'

'You had your revenge, remember?' she responded tautly. 'You fired me and then blackballed me with every business in town. That's excessive even by your standards.'

'I didn't blackball you. I didn't have to. The other construction firms knew what you were without my saying a word, and they avoided you like the plague. My mistake was in not figuring out the truth sooner.' He grabbed her wrist, yanking her close. 'I allowed myself to be seduced by those big black eyes and your soft white skin. But that won't happen again. You can count on it.'

She drew in a panicked breath at his touch, helpless to prevent the sharp, uncontrollable desire that rocketed through her. Did he know? Did he sense her reaction?

She searched his face. Of course he did. The amused curve of his lips, the knowing gleam in his eyes all told her as much. Damn him! 'Let go of me, Damien,' she ordered in an icy voice, drawing back as far as he'd permit.

His grip tightened, and he forced her toward him again until their thighs met, his open suit coat brushing lightly across her breasts. 'Did you really think Leonard Caldwell could give you more than me?' He spoke softly, yet every word stung with biting sharpness. 'Is that why you sold yourself to him?'

She could feel the color drain from her face. 'You know nothing about my reasons for marrying Leonard.' Or did he? Don't let him know about Kyle, she prayed with frantic desperation. Please, don't let him know about our son.

'I know you decided he was the safer bet. I know that you leaked our bids to him. And I know that he married you. Was that the price you held out for? Marriage in exchange for theft?'

'I didn't steal from you!'

'The hell you didn't. I hope it was worth it. Because the time has come to pay for what you took.'

She stiffened, sudden fury overriding every other thought and consideration. 'I've had enough,' she announced. 'I want you out of here. And if you won't go quietly I'll call Security.'

To her consternation, he laughed. 'I don't think so. In fact, you're not moving until you've listened to every word I have to say.'

She attempted to twist from his hold, wincing as his unyielding grasp bruised her wrist. Short of creating a scene, she had little choice but to stand there and hear him out. She shot a swift glance over her shoulder. The other board members were busy availing themselves of the coffee and pastries spread across the buffet table. To her relief, they weren't paying the least attention to her conversation.

Resigned to the inevitable, she turned back to Damien. 'All right, I'm listening. But please let go first. You're hurting me.'

For a minute, she didn't think he'd do it. Then his grip eased and his thumb stroked across the narrow bones of her wrist. 'I'd forgotten how quick you are to bruise,' he said, a hint of regret flickering in his eyes.

'Forget it.' She dismissed his concern. 'I also heal fast.'

His jaw tightened. 'So you do. Thanks for the reminder.'

'What do you want, Damien?' she prompted softly.

His voice turned grim. 'Retribution. Oh, don't look so shocked, Sable. Even you must realize that no one steals from me and gets away with it. I don't take that sort of betrayal sitting down. I'm here to make that point crystal-clear.'

'I swear to you, Damien . . . it didn't happen that way. I didn't steal——'

'Stop it!' He didn't raise his voice. He didn't need to. The fierce expression on his face was more than enough to ensure her silence. 'We went through this five years ago. You can protest all you want, but it won't alter the facts. The leak came from you.'

Her gaze wavered, then fell. He was right. The leak had come from her. But it hadn't happened the way he claimed. It hadn't been deliberate. Not that that changed anything. He believed her guilty of stealing from him. And he didn't intend to listen to any excuses. All she could do was try and find out his intentions and mitigate the damage if possible.

'What do you plan to do?' she whispered.

'I told you. I plan to address your board.'

'About what?' She searched his face apprehensively. 'My marriage to Leonard? Our affair?'

He smiled without humor. 'That, sweet Sable, you'll find out along with the other board members.'

'Do you really think they'll care about our past relationship?' she questioned in disbelief.

He shrugged. 'Perhaps. Perhaps not.'

'What if I refuse your request?' she dared to threaten. 'If I don't permit you to address the board, what then?'

'I wouldn't recommend it,' he advised harshly. 'It will only make your situation worse.'

Worse than what? she wondered in dread. She bit down on her lip. If only she had a few minutes alone to think, to figure out what he might be after. 'I need more time.'

'You're out of time,' he informed her. 'What's your decision?'

She had no choice and they both knew it. She inclined her head. 'Address the board, if you must. But we'll have to wait for Patricia. She seems to be running late today.'

'That won't be necessary.'

'But——'

'Do it, Sable. We don't have time to discuss this further. Cornelius is coming over with our coffee. Now call the meeting to order and introduce me.'

'Don't give me orders. You're not running the show, Damien,' she retorted sharply. 'I am.'

'You are for the time being. That could change, so don't press your luck.'

She caught her breath and took a step away from him, something in his expression warning her not to push him any further. 'Gentlemen,' she announced in a carrying voice, 'if you'll take your seats, Mr Hawke would like to address the board before we begin.'

She took the coffee from Cornelius with a grateful smile and crossed to the head of the conference table. As she stood waiting for everyone to be seated, her gaze settled on a portrait of her late husband. He gazed down at her from the far wall, his smile as kind and gentle as the man had been. She struggled to draw strength from his memory. But it was a futile act.

Leonard had always been the one in need of strength, and she'd always been there to provide it. When he'd fallen ill, she'd assumed more and more of his responsibilities. Just before his death, he'd made his final request—that she protect Caldwell's from the vultures who'd try and steal it after his death, protect his business from corporate raiders... raiders like Damien Hawke.

Taking a deep breath, she turned to face the six board members. 'I've had a rather unusual request. One of our shareholders, Damien Hawke, has asked to address the board before we begin our meeting. I've agreed to his request.' She glanced at him as she took her seat. 'Damien?'

'Excuse the interruption, but what about Patricia?' Cornelius protested. 'I don't think it's appropriate to begin without her.'

'That won't be necessary,' Damien replied. He stood at the end of the rectangular conference table opposite Sable, one hand thrust in his trouser pocket. 'Effective today, Patricia Caldwell is off the board. I've arranged for copies of her letter of resignation to be delivered to each of you.'

No one said a word, identical looks of shock on every face. 'Resigned?' gasped one member. 'But... how?

Why?' His questions broke the silence. Others raised their voices in concern, decorum vanishing beneath sudden, noisy confusion.

'Please.' Sable cut through the babble. 'I believe that's what Mr Hawke intends to explain.'

'Quite right.' His smile of satisfaction said it all, told her all too clearly that her troubles had only just begun. 'Last week Patricia sold me her shares of Caldwell stock. With the public stock I've acquired these past five years, I now control forty-three percent——'

'*Forty-three*! That's more than——'

All eyes turned in Sable's direction. Throughout Damien's remarks, she'd kept carefully quiet, her hands clenched in her lap, struggling to keep from revealing any thought or emotion. Now she stared at Damien across the length of the table. 'What do you want?' she asked one final time. But the question was pointless. Now that it was far too late, she'd finally figured out his intentions.

'What do I want? Why, I want to replace Patricia on the board, of course.' A slow smile crept across his mouth and his eyes bored into hers. 'And I want to replace you as chairman.'

CHAPTER TWO

SABLE thrust back her chair and stood up. 'You can't be serious!'

'I'm dead serious,' came Damien's instant reply.

The others in the room might not have existed. Only the two of them were present, faced off across the room, locked in a not so private battle of wills. Their eyes met, his gaze harsh and relentless, and she knew without question that he wouldn't shift from his stance. He planned to take her down. His rigid posture, his squared jaw, the brilliant light of combat that sparked in his eyes all told her as much. No one could oppose Damien when he was in this mood and win. It wasn't possible. Never had she felt so vulnerable, so threatened.

He'd arranged all the moves beforehand. She'd lost the battle before it had ever begun, before she'd even realized there was a war. And though she'd never known Damien to allow his emotions to affect business decisions she didn't doubt for a minute that this was the exception to the rule. This wasn't just business.

It was personal.

'You can't just waltz in here and take over the board,' she informed him coldly.

'Can't I?' He looked at each board member in turn. 'The general voting public owns seventeen percent of this company. Sable and I, between us, own the rest. I only need eight percent of the outside shareholders voting with me to take over, whereas Sable needs eleven to retain control. If it came to a proxy fight, my name alone would

28

generate the eight percent I require to take over Caldwell's.'

'He's right, Sable,' Cornelius muttered in dismay. 'He won't be able to remove us from the board until the next election, but——'

'But I'll put that six-month wait to good use, soliciting the votes I need,' Damien interrupted. 'By the time the next election comes around I'll have a whole new slate of board members ready and eager to run against you. And we'll win.'

'Our shareholders would never go along with that!' spluttered one of the more junior members.

Damien didn't bother to conceal his contempt. 'Won't they? After the profit statements you've posted for the past two quarters, I'm surprised they haven't already lynched the lot of you.'

'It was Patricia,' Cornelius spoke up. 'She——'

Damien cut him off. 'It doesn't matter who's at fault. The shareholders will blame you. If you fight me, you have my word, by the next election every last one of you will be gone.' He paused, giving them all time to digest his words. 'You'll be gone, unless...'

Sable sank into her chair, knowing that by doing so she'd tacitly relinquished the floor to him. Knowing, too, that her actions would speak far louder than any words. All through his comments she'd listened, trying to decide if there were other options available to them. So far, she couldn't see any. Damien had them over a barrel, and every person in the room had better realize it. Fast.

'Name your terms, Damien,' she said quietly.

'I want to be voted on to the board, effective immediately.'

Her hands clenched in her lap. 'And then?'

'I want the chairmanship.'

Everyone's attention shifted to focus on her reaction, the board members waiting with bated breath, for her response. She forced herself to relax against the upholstered back of her chair, crossing one leg over the other. She didn't dare allow them to see how badly Damien had shaken her. 'I'm out and you're in?' she asked, lifting an eyebrow in amused disbelief. 'Just like that? You know nothing about Caldwell's, nothing about the way it's run, the people who work here. And yet you want to head the company.'

He planted his hands on the table and leaned toward her. 'Are you questioning my abilities? You, of all people?'

Sable shook her head. 'I question neither your experience nor your abilities.' She spoke crisply, assuming her most businesslike demeanor. 'I do question your current knowledge of Caldwell's situation. And I question your ability to make appropriate decisions without the least familiarity with our employees or clients to back them up.'

'I know this business inside and out.' He dismissed her concerns with an arrogant shrug.

She inclined her head. 'I'm aware of that. As our chief competitor you would. But you don't know *Caldwell's* inside and out.' She fixed her dark eyes on him, meeting his fierce green gaze without flinching. 'I do.'

'You know my terms, Sable. Step down,' he growled.

She straightened. 'Hear me out first!'

For one frightening moment, she didn't think he would; she thought that he'd just walk away and make good on his threat. Then he nodded in agreement. He continued to stand at the far end of the conference desk like some warrior of old, his arms folded across his chest, his legs slightly spread and feet planted as though for action. She searched his closed expression for some sign of vulnerability, anxiously hoping to discover some betraying chink in his armor that she could use to her advantage.

She saw nothing.

'You have one minute,' he said. 'Convince me.'

'Very well.' She took a deep breath, marshaling her arguments with as much speed and logic as possible. 'I have no desire to get into a proxy fight with you, nor do I think it will benefit Caldwell's to have a new board, to lose the experience these gentlemen bring to their positions. I suggest a compromise.'

She almost choked offering even that much. But she didn't have any other option. Right now she had to find a way to salvage what she could from this disaster. She had to gain enough time to find a way to fight him...and win. Damn Patricia for creating this mess! She must be laughing her head off, hoping her actions would destroy Sable, perhaps even destroy Caldwell's. Leonard's sister had wanted revenge for having been forced to give up the chairmanship, and she'd taken it... Dear lord, how she'd taken it!

'What's your compromise?' Damien demanded.

'We'll agree to vote you onto the board...'

His mouth curled to one side. 'How kind of you.'

She gritted her teeth. More than anything she wanted to cut loose, to tell him what she really thought and felt. But she didn't dare. Not when he held all the winning cards. 'You own forty-three percent of the stock. It only makes sense that you should have a say in how the company is run,' she conceded.

'And the chairmanship?' The overhead lights picked out the streaks of gold gleaming in his thick tawny hair. He reminded her more than ever of a rogue lion. A rogue lion ready and able to take over her turf, to force his domination.

She took a deep breath. 'Leave the chairmanship in my hands for three months. That will give you time to familiarize yourself with Caldwell's and——'

'One month.'

'But——'

He shook his head, a quiet laugh rumbling deep in his chest. 'Did you think I'd grown soft in the past five years? That I'd stand back and allow you to call the shots? You should know me better than that.'

'I know you, Damien.' The words burst out before she could stop them. 'I certainly know better than to ever call you soft or to think you'd allow anyone to have authority over you. You lead the pack or no one does. Isn't that right?'

A smile touched his mouth and she suspected he found her loss of control humorous. When would she ever learn? she wondered in despair. She couldn't afford to make a single mistake with him. Not now. Not ever.

'That's right. I lead and you follow.' His smile died, his words hard and brutal. 'You're a fool, Sable, if you believe I'd give you three months to scramble for votes or to improve your performance record. If you don't step down at the next board meeting, everyone seated at this table will be gone as of the next election. You have my personal guarantee.'

'I could fight you,' she dared to threaten.

'And you'd lose.'

He was right and they both knew it. Slowly she nodded. Giving in to him had to be one of the most difficult tasks she'd ever undertaken. But she had to be sensible. She had to consider what was best for the board, for her employees, and for the business. Still... She couldn't just let him take it all, give up and walk away. She needed to buy some time.

Her hands tightened into fists and she forced the words past her lips. 'You'll have my decision about the chairmanship at the next meeting.'

His eyes narrowed. 'That's not an answer.'

She lifted her chin. 'It's all the answer you're going to get,' she bluffed, well aware that if he pressed for further concessions she'd be forced to give them to him.

'Hoping to find a loophole, Sable?' he mocked.

'Just covering all the possibilities,' she retorted. 'Wouldn't you, in my position?'

'Without question.' His voice dropped, the sound dark and intimate. 'But just so you know... I haven't left any loopholes. I never do. Whether you realize it yet or not, you're trapped with nowhere to escape. I have you, Sable.'

She couldn't mistake the threat, nor the intense animosity. It poured off him in waves. She stared in shock, fear creeping along her spine like icy fingers. He wasn't just talking about Caldwell's any more. Whether the others seated at the table were aware of it or not, Damien's remarks had turned personal again.

She bit down on her lip. Why was he still so furious, so hostile? Five years should have cooled the fire of his anger somewhat. Or had time merely banked the embers, allowing them to smolder until the perfect opportunity occurred to fan the flames? Still... All this passion over losing those accounts to Caldwell's. It seemed unreasonable. Her eyes widened as a sudden thought occurred to her. Or could it be more than that? Could it be... Kyle? Did he know about their son, after all?

She didn't have the time or energy to consider that possibility. Not now. Not when the entire board was

waiting to see what she'd do next. She fought for
strength, focusing her attention on the board meeting—
and on the unpleasant, though necessary, task ahead.

'Gentlemen,' she announced in a brisk voice, flipping
open the file in front of her. 'Let's cut through all the
rhetoric and get down to business. I hereby call the board
of directors for Caldwell's to order. According to our
by-laws we need an immediate replacement for any board
vacancies. We currently have such a vacancy. All in favor
of Damien Hawke filling that seat, say aye.'

Not a single board member looked at her as they murmured their assent.

'Any nays?' she questioned drily.

No one spoke.

'The motion carries. Mr Hawke, welcome to the
board. Please take a seat.' She didn't give anyone time
to speak, but continued determinedly onward. 'If
everyone will refer to their notes, we'll begin. Damien,
feel free to use Patricia's copy. I'll have another set run
off for you, if you wish. Cornelius, have we any old
business to discuss?'

To her profound relief, he took over from there,
leading the conversation and giving her time to recover.
Through sheer force of will she kept an interested expression on her face, but the exact details of the ensuing
exchange escaped her. All her attention remained fixed
on Damien... on the angled sweep of his cheekbones,
on the strength of his hands as he gestured, on the distinctive timbre of his voice.

It had been so long, so very long, since they'd parted.
So long since she'd been this close to him. Until this
morning, the last time she'd seen him he'd held her naked
in his arms and kissed her with a depth and passion un-
matched by anything she'd experienced before or since.

The memory alone left her shaken, had the power to make her tremble with a soul-crippling need.

She lowered her eyes in dismay. She should be paying attention to the board meeting, not fantasizing about Damien. But she couldn't concentrate. Especially not when she realized that he was watching her as intently as she watched him. He seemed to be biding his time, waiting for... What? Or was he simply absorbed in memories too? Were images of them as they'd once been flashing through his mind? Did he remember as clearly as she their first kiss, the first time they'd made love, that final, wrenching parting?

It wasn't until Cornelius reported on the status of their latest contracts that she awoke to the conversation, the abrupt transition between dreams and reality a brutal intrusion.

'Say that again,' she demanded, more sharply than she'd intended.

'We've lost another project, Sable,' Cornelius explained reluctantly. 'Luther has bailed out on us.'

'Luther! But he's been with us from the start. We built the first three phases of his Walnut Creek development. Why in the world would he walk?'

'We're looking into it, but Matheson is bewildered. They've gone with A.J. Construction and we haven't been able to find out why. At least, not yet.'

'Who is this Matheson?' Damien interrupted.

'He's our project director,' Sable explained tersely.

Damien's frown turned black. 'It must be something critical if Luther's gone over to the competition at the end of such a large development. And your project director has no explanation? None at all?' He spoke with quiet emphasis but from the way the board cringed he might as well have roared the question.

Actually, this wasn't the first client they'd lost, though Sable didn't dare admit as much. The gradual slump in business had begun during Patricia's tenure as chairwoman, a position she'd assumed a year ago, right after Leonard's death. She'd dismissed their concern, saying that it was undoubtedly a temporary condition, one that would correct itself given time. Clearly, she was wrong.

'We're looking into it,' Sable assured him, hoping to end the discussion before it turned acrimonious. She shot Cornelius a speaking look, willing him to pick up on her cues and change the subject.

With a quick nod of understanding, he cleared his throat, speaking hastily. 'Next we have——'

'Hold it. I'm not finished,' Damien cut in. 'And we're not moving on until I'm satisfied with your answers. What are you doing to correct this situation?'

'First we have to find the cause,' Sable explained. 'Once we know why the condition exists, we can take steps to correct it.'

'Thank you, Madam Chairman, but that's apparent even to me.' His sarcasm made her wince. 'What does this Matheson have to say?'

'Nothing,' she replied, her patience beginning to wear thin. 'Yet. As I explained, he's looking into it.'

'Not to my satisfaction, he isn't,' came Damien's immediate retort. 'Did we lose the account because of poor workmanship, inferior materials, cost overruns? What?'

His heated gaze passed over the other board members. To Sable's chagrin, none could meet his eyes, every last one of them becoming engrossed in reading his notes. Damien swore beneath his breath and for the first time that day she shared his feelings. It was hard to respect a board that couldn't answer such basic questions.

'I'll explain the urgency of the situation to Matheson,' she said, in the hopes of easing the situation. 'I'll speak to him today.'

'You do that.' His gaze clashed with hers, his eyes reflecting his contempt. 'I paid a hefty sum for my stock in Caldwell's. I'm not about to sit back and watch my investment go down the tubes due to your shoddy business practices. I want some answers and I want them now.'

'I told you. Matheson's working on it,' Sable tried again.

A muscle jerked in his cheek, a sure sign that he was struggling to keep his fury in check. 'Then he'll work harder. I want a preliminary report from him tomorrow and a comprehensive analysis on my desk by the end of the month. I also suggest that at our next board meeting each of the department heads attend and present reports on their projects and clients in person. I want them available to answer any questions we might have.'

What he really meant was any questions *he* might have, Sable realized. She didn't bother protesting. It would be pointless. He was like a river in full flood, sweeping any opposition aside with stunning force. While she'd been busy dwelling on the past, he'd waited for the perfect moment to take control of the meeting. And from long experience she knew that nothing she could say or do would wrest that control from his grasp.

The rest of the meeting proved as much. He directed the discussions, questioned everything and demanded exhaustive responses. And he cut through the pomposity, forcing the board members to focus on the facts. To Sable's secret amusement, the more recalcitrant of them soon learned that Damien didn't take opposition well. A few choice words tossed in their direction and they fell swiftly into line.

It reminded her of the old days—days when they'd worked side by side, days when observing him bending antagonistic boards to his will had filled her with an intense admiration and excitement. Days long gone.

Throughout the meeting, his challenging gaze came to rest on her with increasing frequency. Was he daring her to protest? Daring her to resist his blatant appropriation of her position? If so, he'd have quite a wait. This wasn't the time. She'd choose her own battlefield. And when the chance came to thwart him she'd seize it with both hands. In the meantime, she'd sit back and watch. Watch for the best opportunity and try and figure out his next move.

'That's the last of it,' Cornelius announced, relief palpable in his voice. 'Sable?'

'If there's nothing further, we're adjourned,' she announced.

Several of the board members thrust back their chairs and stood with alacrity. Sable took her time. Making a final notation, she straightened her papers and slipped the file folder into her briefcase. She sensed Damien's approach, though she refused to look his way. Her lack of response didn't deter him. He planted a hand on her shoulder, his long fingers sliding over her silk jacket and probing the delicate bones beneath.

'Let's go,' he stated without preamble.

She attempted to slip from beneath his hold, but he didn't release her and reluctantly she glanced up, her cheek grazing his hand. The accidental touch sparked an unexpected flash of heat, catching her by surprise. The reaction must have surprised him just as much, for his grip tightened reflexively, his fingers biting deep.

'You want to leave?' she asked, her voice low and husky.

'Yes.' His hold eased, his thumb pressing into the taut muscles along the nape of her neck, massaging the tiny kinks.

She relaxed despite herself, the slow, unrelenting caress provoking a response she'd thought long dead . . . hoped was long dead. She didn't want him touching her, didn't want to feel the heady rush of emotions that that touch inevitably wrought. She wanted to hate him, not—— Her eyes widened.

'We can't go.' She hurried into speech. 'There's a board luncheon after the meeting. We're expected to attend.'

He shook his head. 'Not today. I'm sure everyone will understand that you and I have important matters to discuss. Private matters.'

She tensed beneath his hand. 'I didn't think there was anything more for us to discuss. You've made your desires perfectly clear.'

'Have I?' An enigmatic smile played about his mouth. His fingers drifted upward to stroke the side of her neck and the sensitive area just beneath her jaw. Then his hand fell away, leaving her strangely bereft. 'You're so certain?'

She caught the thread of amusement running through his words and stirred uneasily. Was she wrong? Were the requests he'd made here today only the beginning? What more could he want? She thought of Kyle again, and fear, fierce and primitive, shot through her. Her heartbeat quickened, racing with the desperate, instinctive need to protect her child from harm.

'Damien?' she whispered through numb lips. 'What now? What more could you possibly want?'

'The only way you'll find out is to come with me.' He inclined his head toward the board members clustered in the far corner like a flock of broody hens. 'Make our excuses and let's go.'

She hesitated. 'Go where?'

'To my office.'

She longed to refuse his request. Unfortunately, however, it wasn't a request—it was an order. She debated arguing but, knowing Damien as well as she did, it would prove pointless. He was a man accustomed to getting his way, no matter what it took. Besides, if she wanted to discover what more he expected from her, she'd better take his orders for the time being.

'Give me a moment,' she capitulated with as much grace as she could muster. She joined Cornelius and made her excuses for her abrupt departure. His lack of surprise told her the change of schedule wasn't entirely unexpected.

'Be careful,' Cornelius muttered in an undertone. 'I don't know why, but he has it in for you.'

'You've noticed?' she retorted drily. 'You're right, of course. And I'll be very careful.' Not that it would do her any good. Gathering up her briefcase, she returned to Damien's side. 'I'm ready,' she announced, though it was a blatant lie. She doubted she'd ever be ready for what he had planned.

He didn't reply, simply opened the door and waited for her to walk out of the conference room. She turned automatically in the direction of her office and he fell in beside her. 'Will I need my briefcase?' she asked.

'No. I prefer to keep it casual.' He opened the door to her office and followed her in. 'We'll have lunch and see if we can't hash out the finer details between us.'

The finer details of what? she couldn't help but wonder. She dropped her briefcase on her desk and turned to leave, but he didn't seem in any hurry. Instead he wandered through her domain, examining the few personal pieces she kept at the office. He paused by her credenza and frowned, picking up a lopsided clay vase painted in brash primary colors—Kyle's last birthday present to her. He turned to face her and she stiffened, waiting for the inevitable questions, waiting for his keen intellect to reach what seemed to her such an obvious and logical conclusion.

He flicked the wilted zinnias that drooped over the lip with his fingertip. 'Either you've acquired a liking for primitive art or you're showing unusually poor taste.'

'I like it,' she said, fighting to sound normal. 'Isn't that the most important consideration when it comes to acquiring art?'

'Not according to the investors I know.' To her intense relief, he returned the vase to her credenza, his attention drawn to the simple gold-framed photo pushed to the back of the odd assortment of knickknacks. A bitter smile twisted his mouth. 'Ah. The dearly departed husband. What the hell did you ever see in him?' he questioned, picking up the photo.

'He . . . he was kind.'

'Kind?' Damien's mouth curled. 'He was an insipid fool who fell apart at the first sign of trouble.'

'He was a wonderful businessman,' she insisted, leaping to Leonard's defense.

Damien didn't bother to conceal his contempt. 'His father was a wonderful businessman. Leonard wouldn't have known a blueprint from a spreadsheet. In the few short years he managed the Caldwell empire, he lost everything his father had built up except the con-

struction company. And if good old Lenny had lived
he'd have lost that too.' His expression turned savage.
'Instead, his wife has that honor.'

She paled at the threat. 'Why, Damien? Why did you
go after him? Was it ... because of me?'

'What the hell do you think?'

So it was. She'd suspected as much, but she'd hoped
against hope that she'd been mistaken. Guilt ripped
through her. Hawke Enterprises and Caldwell's had
always been rivals, each a huge conglomerate that spread
into all phases of construction and development. At one
time their rivalry had been a friendly one, but all that
had changed shortly after her ... betrayal and her marriage to Leonard. With methodical calculation Damien
had stripped the Caldwell empire of every holding except
the construction company, bringing the Caldwell family
to the brink of ruin.

And it was largely her fault.

She'd met Patricia Caldwell at a trade show and they'd
struck up a friendly conversation. Of course, she'd been
Patricia Samson then. And Sable had never once connected Patricia Samson, older friend and mentor, with
Patricia Caldwell, cut-throat rival. Well, Sable had paid
for that small mistake. And if Damien's threat was anything to go by, she'd continue to pay.

She took a step back, staring at him as though she'd
never seen him before. 'I can't believe your vindic-
tiveness,' she whispered in an appalled voice. 'You'd
cripple Caldwell's in order to get at me?'

He tossed the photo back on to her credenza, his
amusement a vicious thing. 'You think I took Leonard
down just because of you?'

'You didn't go after him until we married,' she retorted defensively. 'What else should I believe?'

He stalked closer, towering above her, his fury barely held in check. 'Correction. I didn't go after Leonard until you stole for him. He made the first move. All I did was finish the game.'

'That isn't how it happened! Why won't you believe me?'

'You try my temper,' he informed her through gritted teeth. 'Caldwell admitted everything, even if you won't. If he couldn't stomach a fight, he shouldn't have started one. And neither should you.'

'Stop it, Damien!' she said with sharp-edged impatience, her anger rising to match his. 'You keep insisting I stole from you and I keep telling you it wasn't deliberate. I'm guilty of trusting someone I shouldn't have, of exercising poor judgement, I admit it. But I'm not guilty of theft. Never that.'

He folded his arms across his chest, his expression carved into hard, taut lines. 'When did you start playing games, Sable? Or is lying one of your talents, now, too?'

'Patricia was a friend——'

He approached, crowding so close that she could scarcely breathe. 'Such a good friend that you handed her the Anderson account. Then you thought, What the hell? and gave her Vincent Zepher and his chain stores, too.'

She didn't know why she bothered, but she had to try to convince him one final time. 'I didn't know she was Leonard's sister. She was married at the time——'

'And let's not forget that little venture I'd planned for Martinique. They all went to Caldwell's thanks to you.'

'Samson. She said her name was Samson. How was I to know she was related to Caldwell's?'

Before she realized his intention, he snagged her arm, slamming her up against him. 'A year's work! I lost a full year's work. And you? You ended up married to the president of the competition. Now tell me firing you was unjust, that going after Caldwell was out of line.'

'I was indiscreet, I admit that,' she conceded, fighting his hold. 'But I swear to you, it wasn't deliberate.'

He encircled her waist, tugging her into the cradle of his hips. 'You saw a chance for a bigger prize. You put yourself on sale to the highest bidder. And Caldwell paid the price. Marriage in exchange for insider information, isn't that the deal you worked out?'

'No!' She strained away from him, desperate to convince him, more desperate to escape his touch, to escape the unbridled heat of his body. 'No, I swear I didn't betray you. Not like that.'

'Cut the bull, Sable!' One hand snaked up the length of her spine to the back of her head, his fingers thrusting deep into her hair. 'The other execs at the company told me you were the one, but I didn't believe them. It couldn't be you, I said, and I'd prove it.'

She shook her head, tears leaping to her eyes. 'I didn't know what she intended. I swear, I didn't know.'

'So we set a trap. Did you ever figure that out? I gave you false information. Imagine my surprise when Caldwell came in just below that bid—that fictitious bid. I guess Lenny was even more surprised when he lost the contract. Did he ever blame you? He couldn't have, since he married you anyway.' His voice dropped, his words harsh with fury. 'And now, my sweet, it's time to reap your reward for selling me out.'

She froze, the fight draining out of her. 'What do you want?' she whispered apprehensively, her hands splayed across his chest.

'I want you to sell me your shares of Caldwell's.' His smile terrified her. 'But, more than that, I want you back in my bed.' And with that he lowered his head and took her mouth in a fierce, plundering kiss.

CHAPTER THREE

DAMIEN'S kiss was merciless. His mouth crushed Sable's with a dominating force, filled with ruthless male aggression. Shocked to the core, she didn't even think to struggle. Not that she could have. He held her with one powerful arm wrapped around her waist, his fingers biting into her hip and clamping her against the taut, muscular length of him. His other hand was fisted in her hair, tilting her head back to give him complete access to her mouth. And he took full advantage of that access.

He parted her lips, invading the silky warmth within, ravaging with a skill she hadn't experienced in five long years. He knew her so well, knew how to drive her insane with light, teasing caresses, how to rouse her to a fever pitch with deep, passionate strokes, how to carry her so close to the edge that she could only cling to him, pleading desperately for more.

She moaned deep in her throat and in that instant the kiss changed. His embrace was no less forceful, but now he used his familiarity with her to wring a response that she was helpless to suppress. They'd always had an intuitive sense of each other's needs, had used that perception to turn their lovemaking into a joining of monumental proportions. The knowledge that that connection still existed finally shattered her control. She could no more resist him than the tide could resist the pull of the moon.

'Damien, why?' she murmured in a broken voice. Her hands slid up his muscled chest to his shoulders and she clung to him as though her life depended on it.

'I have no choice,' he muttered against her lips. 'And neither do you.'

He kissed her again and this time she opened to him. It was as though a thousand suns had joined together as one. A liquid heat burned through her with white-hot strength, flooding her with an avid hunger, an explosive desire. For too long she'd been forced to suppress her needs. She'd put herself second for years now, playing the various roles demanded of her. Mother. Nurse. Businesswoman. But Damien cut through to the heart of her, to the woman smoldering just beneath the surface, setting free the passions she'd kept so carefully in check.

After an eternity, he eased his mouth from hers. But he didn't release her. His breath fanned her face, hot and rapid. 'Did you respond like this to Caldwell? Tell me you married him for love and not money, Sable. Tell me you aren't a thief. Look at me so I can see the expression in your black eyes when you pervert the truth.'

She bowed her head, his words knifing through her with surgical precision. Their kiss, such a wondrous connection for her, was for him just a means of slipping beneath her guard. Why hadn't she realized? She should have known. 'You bastard,' she whispered. 'Haven't you done enough to me, without this?'

His hand cupped the back of her head, forcing her to meet his gaze. She'd always thought of him as a sophisticate—clever, polished, worldly. But in that instant all she saw was raw male savagery beneath a tailored suit. 'Did Caldwell even know what he was missing?' Damien taunted. 'Somehow I doubt it. But you knew. How was it, Sable? How did you feel when he touched you, kissed you, made love to you? How did it feel to sell yourself, body and soul?'

She fought him then, shoving against his chest. She ignored the wrenching pain as her hair snagged in his fingers, struggling to escape the bruising grip at her waist that held her snug against his loins. 'Let me go! You have no right to say those things to me. I didn't steal from you. I didn't!'

'You're lying.' He caught her wrist in his hands, forcing her arms down to her sides, holding her immobile. 'But right now I don't give a damn.'

'Damien, don't,' she begged, knowing what he intended. But her plea fell on deaf ears. Slowly he lowered his head and captured her mouth once more, drinking as though parched. And to her utter shame she didn't resist. Instead she responded with wild abandon, as though his touch alone gave her the sustenance she needed, gave her life itself.

The sound of the door being flung open behind them resounded through the room like a gunshot. 'Mrs Caldwell? I——' Janine broke off, her horrified gasp revealing the extent of her shock.

This time when Sable attempted to jerk free Damien allowed it. He turned to face the appalled secretary. 'Don't you know how to knock?' he demanded, his fury causing the color to drain from Janine's face.

'I'm sorry! I—I——' Janine's pale blue eyes glinted behind her glasses.

Sable struggled to catch her breath. 'What do you want, Janine?' she asked gently.

'The—the letters you asked me to transcribe. They're ready for your signature. Mrs Caldwell, I   you——'

'Leave them on your desk and go ahead to lunch. I'll sign them later.'

'And knock next time,' Damien practically growled.

'Yes, sir!' Janine murmured, and scurried from the office.

The minute the door closed, Sable faced the bank of windows and wrapped her arms about her waist. What a disaster. Janine had been fiercely loyal to Leonard, her devotion bordering on the obsessive. Without question she'd see the embrace as a defection on Sable's part. Would she understand? It shouldn't matter, but somehow it did.

'I didn't mean for there to be witnesses,' Damien said, his approach unnervingly silent.

Knowing him, it was as close to an apology as she'd get. Her mouth curved into an ironic smile. 'Interesting phrasing,' she murmured, turning to face him. 'You don't say, I didn't mean for that to happen. No. You say, "I didn't mean for there to be witnesses." Tell me, Damien, does that imply you planned our little embrace from the start?'

He shrugged, his expression giving no clue as to his thoughts. 'The kiss was inevitable. You know that as well as I.'

'Perhaps.' She didn't bother to argue the point. 'But it's not appropriate at the office.' Reconsidering her comment, she laughed, the sound empty of humor. 'Now that I think about it, it's not appropriate, period.'

'Isn't it?' He sounded indifferent, though his gaze told a different story. It swept over her, his dark green eyes smoldering with barely tamped desire. 'Your hair's come undone,' he told her softly. 'No, don't bother fixing it. I like it that way. It goes with the rest of you.'

Her hands froze halfway to her head. 'What does that mean?'

He smiled in satisfaction. 'No lipstick, mouth swollen from my kisses, cheeks still flushed with passion, blouse half-open. You look...alive, instead of like every other businesswoman in this city.'

Her hands flew to her buttons. When had that happened? Oh, lord. Was that how Janine had seen her? Sable swallowed the nervous knot in her throat and lifted her chin. 'Then you'll have to excuse me while I freshen up.'

Before she could move toward the bathroom, a light tap sounded at the door that separated her office from Patricia's and he shook his head. 'Sorry. You don't have time. Lunch is ready.' Ignoring her protests, he caught her hand in his and drew her across the room toward the door.

'But that leads to——'

'My office.'

Of course. She didn't know why she hadn't realized it sooner. Without a doubt, she could once again thank Patricia for this latest development. When he'd said they'd go to his office, she'd assumed he meant at his Embarcadero headquarters. It had never occurred to her that he meant right next door.

'We're eating in here?' she asked, and then caught her breath as she stepped into the room.

Gone were the hideous animal heads and pelts. Gone was the malodorous clash of perfume and tobacco. Gone was the heavy, pretentious furniture. Even the carpet had been changed from cardinal-red to a misty green. Splashes of taupe and rust and forest-green gave the room color and warmth. And huge ficus trees, palms and colorful birds-of-paradise plants filled each corner, a sure sign that Lute lurked somewhere in the background.

'Where is he?' she demanded, forgetting everything but her need to see Lute.

'Here, Miss Sable.'

She spun round with a cry of delight. Lute stepped from the balcony bearing an empty tray. Setting it on Damien's desk, he held his hands out to her. She didn't hesitate. She hurried to his side and gave him a hug and kiss, even though she knew such demonstrativeness embarrassed him.

'I've missed you,' she said, tears springing unexpectedly to her eyes.

'And I you,' his gruff voice rumbled in her ear. He pushed her gently away and examined her face with a critical eye. 'Shadows,' he murmured with a sad shake of his head. 'Still so many shadows.'

She frowned in bewilderment. 'What are you talking about? What shadows?'

He didn't answer her question. Instead he stroked his narrow beard and lifted a bushy white eyebrow. 'You are hungry, yes? Your lunch is waiting on the balcony.'

Damien stepped forward. 'Thank you, Lute.'

Lute's reserve returned, falling about him like a cloak, his manner once more formal and correct. 'Will there be anything else?'

'Perhaps later.'

Lute picked up the tray and inclined his head. 'Very good. Enjoy your lunch.'

'I'm glad he's still with you,' Sable said as they stepped out on to the balcony. She skirted the small linen-covered table set intimately for two and crossed to the stucco half-wall that overlooked California Street.

Damien lifted an eyebrow. 'Where else would he go?'

'I don't know,' she admitted, fingering the colorful impatiens blossoms filling the planters topping the wall.

Far below a trolley bell rang out, attempting to clear a path as it fought its way through the heavy summer foot traffic. 'From what little he's said, I gather he doesn't have any family. Except you, of course.' She looked over her shoulder at him. 'He's been with you for a long time, hasn't he?'

'Since I was nineteen.' He joined her, resting a hip against the wall, his back to the view. Bright sunshine streaked through his hair, glinting in the browns and golds, dancing off the occasional russet strands. 'Why the sudden curiosity?'

'I've always been curious about Lute. But...' she shrugged '...I never wanted to offend him by asking questions about his past.' She shot Damien a mischievous glance. 'So I'll offend you instead. How did you meet?'

She didn't think he'd answer—during the years she'd known him it had been a taboo subject. But, almost pensively, he said, 'Lute saved my life.'

Sable suppressed a tiny gasp. 'Saved your life? How?'

'In a barroom fight. I was...wild. Crazy. And very drunk. I started an argument in some dive over in West Oakland. Not a smart move.'

'You went to a bar in West Oakland?' She couldn't picture it. He'd never talked much about his background. But she'd always imagined he'd come from a wealthy family—a degree from Stanford didn't come cheaply. 'And they served you liquor when you were only nineteen? That's illegal.'

'So's using a fake ID.'

She tilted her head to one side, a teasing smile playing about her lips. 'What were you doing, slumming?'

It was the wrong question. She realized it the minute she spoke. His face closed over, sudden irritation slashing deep lines from his cheekbones to the taut corners of his mouth. His eyes narrowed, the green like chips of ice. 'What would you know about slumming?' he bit out. 'You've always had everything handed to you.'

'That's not true!' she denied, stunned by the sudden attack. 'I've worked for what I have.'

'Is that what marriage to Lenny was? Work?' She flinched from the bitter cynicism in his gaze. He reached out then, snagging the silk lapel of her jacket with his index finger. 'Let me guess what sort of work.'

She jerked free, outrage bringing a hot rush of color to her cheeks. 'You know nothing of my life with Leonard. Nothing!'

'And you know nothing of my background,' he retorted pointedly.

She caught the implication and frowned in concern, her anger fading as she reconsidered her assumptions. From his reaction to her comment, she must be very wrong about his background. Which suggested he hadn't been slumming. And if that was the case, then ... 'What in the world were you doing in that bar, Damien?' she asked softly.

He didn't avoid the question as she suspected he would. 'I suppose I was trying to kill myself,' he answered, and straightened. 'You ready to eat?'

'Eat?' She stared at him, stunned. 'No, I'm not ready to eat. What do you mean you were trying to kill yourself? Why? How?'

He wasn't going to answer, she could tell. 'I think that's a story for another time,' he said, confirming her suspicion.

As fruitless as she knew it would prove to be, she couldn't let the subject drop. 'What about Lute?' she asked. 'Will you tell me that much of the story?'

She could see the tension tightening the muscles across his shoulders and chest. His hands closed into fists, though his voice remained amazingly dispassionate. 'One of my attackers had a tire iron. Lute took the blow meant for me. If it had landed, I'd be dead. Instead Lute had his forearm shattered and his skull cracked open. He spent three months in a coma. When he woke up he'd lost his memory.'

'He didn't remember the attack?'

A strange smile played about his mouth. 'Oddly enough, that was the one thing he did recall. At least, he remembered me. Except for that brief moment in time, his past was a blank. Who he was, where he'd come from, even his name, had all been wiped clean.'

'But he has a name...'

'Lute was the first word that passed his lips after he woke. We never have found out what it means or its importance, if any. But it...stuck.'

Her brows drew together. 'And he's been with you ever since? You've never been able to find out anything more about his past?'

'He's happy with the life he has.'

It didn't quite answer her question, but she didn't see any point in pressing. 'Why didn't you tell me about this before?' she asked.

'Lute likes his privacy.'

She gazed at him in bewilderment. 'But you've told me now. Why, after all these years?'

He crossed to the table and removed the covers from the platters. 'I only tell his story if he wants it told.'

It took a few seconds for the full significance of that to sink in. Though once it had it left Sable more confused than ever. For some reason, Lute had allowed

Damien to reveal his story. But why now, after all this time?

'Let it go, Sable,' Damien insisted, an impatient edge to his words. 'It's getting late and I still have a lot of work to accomplish this afternoon. Let's have lunch and get down to business. That's why we're here, remember?'

'I remember,' she retorted, stung. 'But it's not like we're complete strangers. We have a past——'

'That's unfortunate, I agree,' he cut her off with cool precision. 'But I have neither the time nor the inclination to dwell on that past. And I wouldn't think you'd want to, either.'

Heartless bastard! How could he say that, as though all their memories were painful ones? 'You're right,' she managed to say, holding her head high, 'I don't.'

Without another word, she took the seat he held out for her, determined to keep all further conversation strictly business. Despite the awning that shaded them, the warmth of the midday July sun made it too hot for a jacket and she removed it. Damien followed suit, shedding his own jacket and loosening his tie. Next he unbuttoned the cuffs of his shirt and rolled them up his forearms to expose the Rolex she'd given him for his thirty-fifth birthday.

She lowered her eyes to hide her reaction, stunned that he still wore it. They'd been in Hawaii at the time, celebrating the finalization of the Simpson deal. He'd been astonished when she'd handed him the gift box and she'd found it highly amusing that he'd forgotten it was his birthday. What had followed had been one of the most treasured nights of her life. He'd carried her out to the rock pool behind the house they'd rented and made love to her beneath the stars, made love to her as though they

were the only two people left on earth and that moment
the only moment that mattered.

She bit down on her lip. Would she ever forget their
years together? Would she at least come to view them
with dispassion? Somehow she doubted it. No matter
how Damien regarded the past, no matter how much he
wanted to dismiss its importance, it linked them with
bands as unbreakable as time itself.

'Wine?'

Her gaze jerked up to meet his. 'What?'

'Here.' He poured her a glass of Riesling. 'You look
like you could use this. Where were you, Sable?'

'Hawaii,' she admitted, seeing no point in lying. She
accepted the glass, her fingers gripping the stem so tightly
that she feared it would snap off in her hand. 'Your
watch,' she added as an explanation. 'It reminded me
of Hawaii.'

His eyes narrowed, but, 'Drink the wine,' was all he
said.

She didn't normally indulge during the day, but something in his expression demanded compliance and she
took a hasty sip. It was delicious, light and tangy with
a fruity aftertaste. 'Why do you still wear it?' she questioned, aware that she was treading on dangerous
ground, but not caring. So much for sticking to business.

'It works.'

Well, she'd asked for it. What had she expected? For
him to declare his undying devotion? She picked up her
silverware and fixed her attention on the plate in front
of her, infuriated by the sudden tears that blurred her
vision. He must have sensed her loss of control for his
wine glass slammed on to the table.

'Stop it, Sable! Stop the games. I gave you everything. Everything! And you chose to betray me. You left

my arms and ran straight into Caldwell's. What I offered wasn't enough for you, was it? Lenny had more and so you gambled on him. Gambled and lost.'

'That's not true.' She looked up, heedless of the tears glittering in her eyes. 'I didn't turn to him until much later. He offered me a job when no one else would. I was desperate. I couldn't get work. The bills were mounting.'

'Don't hand me that. You couldn't have been all that desperate. I know for a fact you had a ring on your finger withins weeks of leaving me.'

'Six weeks,' she said in a hopeless voice. The day after she'd discovered she was pregnant, to be precise. Leonard had insisted they marry when she'd informed him of her condition and she'd been in such a state of shock, so emotionally distraught, that she hadn't the energy to put up much of an argument. In truth, she just hadn't cared.

'You never did go back to work,' he continued. 'Not until Lenny was on the verge of bankruptcy and you had no other choice.'

There was a reason why she hadn't continued working. She'd been obviously pregnant by then, and, afraid that someone would suspect the baby was Damien's, she'd spent the months after her marriage secluded in Leonard's house awaiting Kyle's birth... and missing Damien with an intensity that had wiped every other thought and consideration from her head. Afterward, she'd remained home caring for Kyle because Leonard had preferred it that way, and she hadn't been in much of a position to argue. In fact, it wasn't until his business had been in a shambles and he'd fallen too ill to continue on his own that she'd convinced him to let her help.

'Marrying Leonard was a last resort.' She despised the hint of entreaty that crept into her voice, but she couldn't seem to help it. 'I phoned you countless times, but you wouldn't take my calls, wouldn't see me.'

'What was the point?' he demanded. With a sharp expletive, he thrust back his chair and crossed to the stucco wall. He stood with his back to her, his shoulders stiff and straight beneath his crisp white shirt. 'I didn't trust myself to see you. I was rather…angry at the time.'

He stared down at the street corner far below, his jaw set in an uncompromising line, but she knew he didn't see the jugglers and pantomimists performing for the summertime crowds. He'd turned inward where she couldn't follow, revisiting some long-ago memory. She sensed he fought to keep his control, to maintain his distance emotionally. It was a distance he'd successfully held on to all through the years they were together, a distance that had threatened to destroy their relationship. It very well might have, if Patricia hadn't succeeded first.

'You didn't trust me, Damien. In all the years we were together, you never let me in, never once let down your guard.' She left the table and crossed to his side, daring to rest a hand on his arm. He shoved his fist into his pocket, his biceps bunching beneath her fingers. 'If you'd truly loved me, you'd have known I could never have betrayed you. And you would have moved heaven and earth to help prove my innocence.'

He didn't look at her as she'd hoped. His face remained a stony mask, revealing none of his thoughts. A sudden breeze whipped his hair from his brow, drawing her attention to his profile, to the arrogant sweep of his cheekbones, and to the full, sensuous mouth and squared, determined chin. A muscle jerked in his jaw.

'You married Caldwell. That told me everything I needed to know.'

'There was a reason!' she protested urgently. 'I——'

'Enough!' His control finally snapped, anger consuming him, the anger an even more persuasive deterrent than his icy reserve. He faced her then, his hands closing on her upper arms. 'You made your choice. You chose Caldwell. Now you have another choice to make. Let's hope you show more sense with this one.'

She refused to shrink from his fury, to allow him to intimidate her. 'What are you talking about?'

His eyes glittered with ruthless intent. 'Caldwell's. I want it and you're going to give it to me.'

'I'm supposed to simply hand my shares over to you and walk away?' she demanded in disbelief. 'Just like that?'

His thumbs began a relentless circling, smoothing the ivory silk of her shirt over her arms. 'No, not just like that. I'll pay you for your stock.'

'But at well below market price,' she guessed, struggling not to shiver beneath his touch.

He inclined his head. 'Very astute, Sable. There's also one other condition.'

Something in his tone warned her that she wouldn't like this latest stipulation and she stiffened. 'What is it?'

'I want you in my bed again.'

Her eyes widened and she fought her breath, unable to believe what she'd just heard. 'You can't be serious!'

'I'm dead serious.'

She shook her head, struggling to slip from his grasp. But he held her close, forcing her to face him. 'No, I won't! What makes you think I'd agree to something like that?'

His smile was cold...heartless. 'You'll agree. I promise you, you'll agree. Because if you don't I'll make your life a living hell. And after all the years we worked together you know I'm capable of it.'

'I know all too well,' she shot back.

He laughed in genuine amusement. 'Then you also know I'll do it.'

'But why?' The cry broke from her, filled with anger and hurt. 'Why are you doing this?'

His laughter died, replaced by grim intent. 'Have you any idea how much you cost my firm when you sold out to Caldwell's? It wasn't just a year's work you stole. People lost their jobs. Worse, it became common knowledge that there was a leak, which meant that I lost people's trust. And that, my love, is going to cost you.'

She didn't bother arguing, explaining her error in judgement yet again. If he hadn't listened earlier, he certainly wouldn't listen now. Besides, Caldwell's wasn't her only concern. She had Kyle's welfare to think of. If he ever found out they'd had a son together, he'd have the perfect weapon to use against her—a much more potent and damaging weapon than Caldwell's. And, considering how badly he wanted retribution for past wrongs, it was a weapon he wouldn't hesitate to use. Still... To sleep with him...

'I won't do it,' she whispered. It would kill her to be held in his arms again, to give in to his passion, knowing all the while that he took her for revenge instead of for love. 'I won't sell myself to you.'

He lifted an eyebrow. 'Why not? You sold yourself to Caldwell.'

She flinched, every scrap of color draining from her face. In a sudden twisting move, she jerked free of his arms and stepped back, wrapping her arms around her

waist. It was as though he'd shattered something precious
deep inside of her. Something irreplaceable. A treasure
beyond price.

'Sable——'

She shook her head, raising her hand to hold him at
bay. 'Don't say any more, Damien. Don't say another
word. Just stay away from me.' To her relief, he made
no attempt to touch her, but he watched her as though
concerned. Concerned? She closed her eyes. Not a
chance. He'd just proved how little he cared.

His cruelty actually had a salutary effect, she discovered. It killed all emotion, laying bare her choices.
Choices she needed to weigh carefully. Damien didn't
know about Kyle. He couldn't, not when she logically
analyzed all he'd done and said so far. Which meant
that he'd only come after her to get his hands on
Caldwell's and exact some petty revenge. Well, he could
have his revenge. If it would protect her son, then she'd
give it to him without hesitation. For the longer Damien
remained in her life, the greater the chances that he'd
find out about Kyle. And that was one risk she couldn't
afford to take—no matter what the personal cost.

She opened her eyes and looked at him with unwavering resolve. 'If I sell, and I stress the word "if",
will that end things between us?'

'What do you mean?'

'If I agree to your...''conditions'', will you leave me
alone?' Her voice trembled, but she couldn't seem to
control it. Not when it took every ounce of her will-
power just to stand here and make such a heartrending
offer. 'Will you get out of my life and stay out, per-
manently. Never contact me again, never phone or...or
see me?'

He stilled, eyeing her with a predatory watchfulness that terrified her. She could practically see him analyzing her request, seeing the hidden meaning beneath the surface words. 'What are you up to, Sable?' he murmured.

'Having you appear in my life so unexpectedly is ... is distracting,' she invented with a swiftness born of desperation. 'I want to make sure it doesn't happen again. I want to get on with my life without having to look over my shoulder to see what you're up to. Is that such an unreasonable request?'

'And in exchange for my leaving you alone you'll sell me Caldwell's at a cut rate? You'll sleep with me?'

She shrugged, the movement stiff and unnatural ... revealing. 'Even at a cut rate I'll have more money than I can ever spend. Of course, I'd need time to consider the rest of your offer, but I think we can come to terms.' She shot him a warning glance. '*If* you consent to my stipulation.'

'So agreeable. I wonder why...?' He caught her chin in his hand, tilting her head so that she couldn't avoid his gaze. 'What are you hiding?'

'N-nothing! I'm not hiding anything.'

'Liar,' he accused softly. 'You should be fighting me tooth and nail. Instead you're rolling over in defeat.'

'Is that what you want? A fight?' She turned her head to the side and his fingers slid along her jaw with tantalizing gentleness before dropping away. 'Sorry to be so uncooperative. But, as you've already pointed out, I know you, Damien. And I know what you're capable of. Why should I put myself through that? It doesn't make sense.'

'All very logical,' he conceded. 'But somehow I don't quite buy it. I can see the panic in your eyes, Sable. In your face. Tell me what you're hiding.'

'I'm not hiding anything,' she lied frantically. 'Do you want Caldwell's or don't you? I'd think you'd be pleased that I'm giving in, giving you what you want.'

He glanced away, effectively concealing his thoughts from her. 'You're right, of course,' he said after an endless minute. 'We'll finalize the details tomorrow.'

'And if I sell you'll stay out of my life from then on?' She wanted that point crystal-clear.

'I'll see to it that our paths never cross again ... if you sell.' He looked at her then, his eyes alive with both threat and promise. '*And* if you sleep with me.'

Dear lord, what had she just agreed to? She might as well have signed her own death warrant. 'Fine.' She took a hasty step back, then another and another. If she didn't escape soon, she'd crack wide open, ruining everything. 'If you'll excuse me, I have work to do.'

'You haven't eaten,' he pointed out.

She glanced at the table and quickly away, her stomach churning. She couldn't face eating with him, couldn't handle exchanging polite, meaningless conversation. Not after all he'd done. 'Please make my excuses to Lute. It would seem I've lost my appetite.' And with that she turned and bolted, aware of his intent green eyes boring into her back every inch of the way.

By the time Sable arrived home, she could barely put one foot in front of the other. She tossed her briefcase on to the living-room couch, her shoulders drooping from a combination of exhaustion and stress.

'Mommy!' an excited voice called from the stairway—
a voice that brought her more joy and happiness than
she'd ever thought possible.

She turned, weak tears trembling on the ends of her
lashes. 'Kyle,' she called, dropping to her knees as he
raced into the room. An instant later she held an armful
of heaven to her breast. She closed her eyes, resting a
cheek on the top of his head. His thick dark hair tickled
her nose and she smiled, relaxing for the first time that
day. She could face any adversity, overcome any ob-
stacle, so long as she had him to come home to each
day.

'You're late,' he accused, wriggling free of her embrace and tugging at the pajama bottoms that threatened
to slide down his narrow hips.

'I'm sorry, sweetheart. But I'm home now. Have you
had dessert?' She held out a hand. 'Why don't we
scrounge some milk and cookies from the kitchen and
you can tell me all about your day?'

He hesitated, his teeth worrying at his bottom lip.
'Nanna said no more,' he confessed with a reluctant sigh,
clearly torn between being honest and receiving the unexpected treat.

'I'll tell Nanna it's OK,' she assured him solemnly.

'OK,' he agreed, and grinned, reminding her with
heartbreaking suddenness of Damien.

For the first time she blessed the fact that he'd in-
herited her coloring. During the pregnancy she'd prayed
for a child with tawny hair and vivid green eyes, and
though his features were the image of Damien's they were
hidden beneath a mop of ebony curls and flashing black
eyes. Only under close scrutiny could she see the familiar squared jaw and high, sweeping cheekbones. Even
the wide, sculpted mouth was identical to his father's.

DAY LECLAIRE   65

He slipped his fingers into hers and tugged at her hand.
'Come on!' he urged, and she allowed herself to be towed
in the direction of the kitchen.

Maybe it was listening to Kyle's childish chatter or her
intense exhaustion. Perhaps it was the pain of seeing
Damien again and realizing how thoroughly he despised
her. She never quite knew what decided her, but halfway
through her second chocolate-chip cookie she reached a
decision.

Tomorrow she'd go in and talk to Damien. She'd insist
that they come to terms. She'd agree to sell him her
interest in Caldwell's at whatever price he offered—she'd
even consent to sleeping with him. She'd do anything he
asked, if only he promised to stay out of her life. She
gazed down at the top of her son's head and caught her
breath. To protect Kyle... That was worth far more than
her Caldwell stock. She closed her eyes, fighting to hold
her tears at bay.

It was even worth more than her pride and self-respect.

CHAPTER FOUR

KNOWING she wouldn't get a wink of sleep, Sable spent the entire night planning her speech, marshaling her arguments, and considering all possible alternatives. The next morning she wasted no time, but went directly to Damien's office, prepared to negotiate her release. Pushing open the connecting door, she stared in frustration at the empty room.

He wasn't there.

A small sound caught her attention and she turned to discover an attractive blonde standing by Damien's credenza, her arms loaded with files. 'May I help you?' the woman asked.

Sable nodded. 'Perhaps you can. I'm Sable Caldwell. I'd hoped to speak to Damien.'

'It's a pleasure to meet you, Mrs Caldwell.' The woman put down the files and offered her hand. 'I'm Lisa, Mr Hawke's secretary. I'm afraid he won't be in today.'

'He won't...?' Sable could only stare. 'But I'm supposed to meet with him.'

Lisa stirred uncomfortably. 'Yes, Mrs Caldwell. He mentioned you might stop by. He said that you could call him if it was urgent, but he'd prefer to put your meeting on hold until tomorrow.'

'Tomorrow...?' Sable's mouth snapped closed. She refused to reveal the extent of her outrage, refused to utter the words trembling on the tip of her tongue. He'd done this deliberately. He knew they were supposed to get together, to discuss terms. And he had to guess, even if he didn't know for certain, how anxious she'd be about this meeting. Undoubtedly this was one more way to torture her, to keep her off-balance. 'Thank you, Lisa,' she managed to say in gracious tones. 'It's not in the least urgent. I'll speak to him tomorrow.'

'Yes, Mrs Caldwell,' Lisa murmured, and, with a final uncertain glance over her shoulder, went back to sorting the files.

Stifling a sigh, Sable returned to her office and shut the door. How thoroughly deflating. She crossed to her desk and collapsed into her chair. Swiveling to face the windows, she stared blindly at the San Francisco skyline. Had he known she would have a speech all prepared, would be determined to battle for better terms? Probably. He had an unerring instinct for reading people and had used it to stunning effect during the years she'd worked for him. Now he was using that instinct in his dealings with her. It was incredibly unsettling.

A light tap sounded at her outer door and Ryan Matheson, Caldwell's project director, stuck his head in. 'Excuse me, Sable,' he said. 'Do you have a minute?'

She swung around and smiled. 'Of course. Come in and have a seat. What can I do for you?'

'This is rather awkward,' he began, clearly ill at ease.

If Damien was involved—and she didn't doubt for a minute that he was—she suspected it would prove to be very awkward indeed. 'Sit down, Ryan. I assume this is about the report Damien requested.'

He sank into the chair in front of her desk. 'Yes, it is. Mr Hawke spoke to me at length about Caldwell's having lost the final phases of Luther's condo development and asked that I prepare a report accounting for his defection.'

Reading between the lines, Sable imagined Damien had done a lot more than just speak to Ryan. Chewed him out was more likely. 'He's very concerned about the situation,' she said in classic understatement.

Ryan ran a distracted hand through his rumpled brown hair. 'As am I. The problem is, Luther isn't the only job we've lost in the last year. Though until recently I seemed alone in my concern——' He broke off, shooting her a nervous glance. 'Miss Caldwell said...well...'

Patricia had told him not to press the matter, she guessed, hoping perhaps that ignoring the situation would make it go away. 'That's no longer the case,' Sable explained gently. 'The entire board supports Damien's request.'

'I'm relieved to hear it.' He cleared his throat. 'Which is why I came directly to you.'

She frowned in bewilderment. 'I'm not sure I understand, Ryan. What's the problem?'

He fidgeted, clutching a sheaf of papers between sweaty hands. 'Well...I've spoken to Luther a number of times, trying to pin down the real reason for his jumping ship, asking if there was anything we might have done that could be responsible for his switching to A.J. Construction. I mean, I've looked at everything—costs, workmanship, materials, union problems. The works. And there's nothing there. Except...'

'Except?' she prompted, completely mystified by his nervousness.

'Yes... Well...' He fingered his collar, then broke into speech. 'Except that they turned down our bid. It was sorta peculiar. Very last-minute. One day we had it in the bag and the next day we were out.'

'I don't suppose you could be more specific?' she asked, struggling to conceal her exasperation. 'What do you suspect happened?'

He looked at her, then quickly away. 'I think we were underbid.'

She didn't understand his nervousness. 'That happens all the time in this business, doesn't it? I mean, it's unfortunate, but——'

'It doesn't happen. At least, not like this,' Ryan cut in abruptly. 'We built the first three phases for Luther. That alone should practically guarantee our getting the final contract. Plus, they're not admitting to any problems with the actual construction. In fact, we've met all our deadlines and come in under budget. So why dump us? It doesn't make sense. Our site manager is still in shock. He can't explain the sudden switch. I mean, we were caught flat-footed. And... and there have been rumors.'

'What sort of rumors?' she asked uneasily.

'Rumors of a leak.'

'A *leak*?' She jackknifed upright in her chair, staring in disbelief. 'There must be some mistake.'

He cleared his throat. 'There's no mistake. From what I hear A.J. Construction didn't just underbid us, they walked in with our package in one hand and a list of bargains and perks in the other. They offered a better deal on every aspect of the project, using our prospectus as a guideline.' His gaze flitted about the room, never once settling on her. 'As you know, that information is supposed to be highly confidential. I can't explain how they got hold of it, but I thought you should be made aware of the problem since my report to Mr Hawke... I hope you understand... I really have no choice, given the situation.'

Icy tendrils of dread snaked through her, settling like a lead weight in the pit of her stomach. 'You're telling me that the possibility of a leak will figure prominently in your report?'

He finally looked at her, the hint of pity in his expression impressing on her the seriousness of the situation more clearly than anything he'd said to date. 'That's precisely what I'm telling you.'

'I appreciate the warning.' She fought to think, to scramble for a plan of action. How was this possible? If Ryan was right, who could be responsible? A sudden thought occurred to her. 'I'd like a list of all personnel who had access to this bid information.'

'Everyone?' he asked.

She didn't hesitate for a minute. 'Every last person, including you and me.' She leaned forward, leveling her gaze on the project director. 'Assuming there has been a leak, I want to find out who is responsible, and fast—if possible, before that report hits Damien's desk.'

He eyed her suspiciously for several long minutes, as though assessing her sincerity. Slowly he relaxed. 'I'll draw up the list,' he said, but then a note of apprehension crept into his voice. 'Sable, you'd better know. The facts won't be easy to refute. And suspicion is going to fall on the most obvious target. And I don't have to tell you who that would be.'

Her eyes widened. No, he didn't. His expression said it all. If she didn't find out who had leaked the information, she'd hang for it based on past history alone. And Damien would be first in line with the lynching rope. Panic threatened to overwhelm her. Her hands curled into fists, her nails biting into her palms. She had to calm down and think. First things first. 'When will you complete your final report?' she questioned tautly.

'Mr Hawke said to have it on his desk by the end of the month. That gives you three weeks.' He lowered his voice. 'Three weeks, assuming we don't lose any more contracts the way we lost this one. If we do... Sable, when this comes out, the board's going to ask some tough questions——' He broke off, staring miserably at the floor. 'And you'd better have the right answers.'

'I understand.' It was a lie. She didn't understand at all. 'And Ryan?'

He looked up. 'Yes.'

'Thank you.'

'I'm... I'm sorry.' He stood up. 'If there's anything else I can do...'

She inclined her head. 'You'll be the first to know.'

The minute the door closed behind him, she reached for the phone and put a call through to Alex Johnson, president of A.J. Construction. To her frustration, he was out until late that afternoon, but his assistant promised to relay the urgency of her message. The rest of the day she spent liaising with Ryan Matheson in an attempt to draw up a list of possible suspects.

The very act made her physically ill.

By six that night Sable had reached the end of her rope. She closed her eyes and leaned back in her chair, forced to concede temporary defeat. She'd gone over and over the list that she and Ryan had formulated. Every last name on it was someone she trusted and respected. What in heaven's name was she supposed to do next? How could she uncover the truth? The phone rang at her elbow and she snatched it up, praying it would be Alex.

'Johnson here,' the caller announced abruptly. 'You phoned, Mrs Caldwell?'

'You can't be surprised to hear for me,' she commented, deciding to get right down to business. Why waste time on pleasantries when not one aspect of this whole situation was in the least pleasant? 'Not once news of the leak... leaked.'

He laughed, a great booming sound of genuine amusement. 'I guess not. Certain individuals at Caldwell's must be major league ticked about that. Snatched Luther right from under your noses, didn't we?'

'With a little help,' she said drily.

'Is that what you're calling about?'

'Of course.'

'You want me to keep my—er—source confidential, is that it?'

Her brows drew together. 'No! I want you to tell me where you got your information. Who gave you the copy of our prospectus?'

A long moment of silence greeted her response. 'This is some sort of joke, right?'

'No, it's not a joke,' she snapped. 'You have the Luther project and nothing's going to change that. But, as a businessman, you can appreciate our predicament, I'm sure. We need to find the source of your information. Are you willing to help us?'

'Are you taping this call?'

'No, of course not.'

'Are we on speakerphone or something?'

'Our conversation is completely confidential. No one even knows I've called you.'

'Then you're wasting your breath.'

'You won't tell me who's responsible for giving you a copy of our bid?'

'You already know who give us the information.' He spoke sharply, impatiently.

She sighed in frustration. 'Mr Johnson, if I already knew, I wouldn't be calling you, now would I?'

'I'd say that depended.'

'Depended on what?'

'On whether you were hoping this call would cover your backside. Why the game, Mrs Caldwell? *You* gave us Caldwell's prospectus. Did you think I hadn't been told? Use your head, woman! I'm the one who authorized that hefty little sum we paid you. So quit wasting my time with pointless phone calls. And don't bother me again unless you have more information you want to sell.'

'No, wait! Please!'

It was too late; he'd already hung up. The receiver fell from her hand, clattering into the cradle. He thought she'd sold him the information, she realized in disbelief. But...how? She didn't understand any of this. How could he think she was to blame? Could someone be using her name? If so, who? And why? A sob caught in her throat and she pressed trembling fingers to her mouth, fighting the urge to break down and weep. What in heaven's name was she to do now?

'Sable?'

She jumped, a soft cry escaping before she could prevent it. Damien stepped from the shadows and she stared at him with huge, panicked eyes. 'You startled me,' she managed to say.

He removed his suit coat and loosened his tie, his green eyes watchful. 'What's wrong, Sable?'

'Nothing. Why...why do you ask?'

'Your phone call. From what little I overheard you sounded rather desperate. And you look...' He tilted his head to one side, his brows drawing together. 'You look frightened. What is it? What's wrong?'

For an insane moment, she considered telling him everything, throwing herself on his mercy and begging for help. She stopped herself just in time. How could she have forgotten, for even one tiny minute, that Damien had no mercy? To hand him the information about A.J. Construction would be as good as insuring her own destruction. It would be just the weapon he'd need to ruin her completely. And she didn't doubt for one minute that he'd take full advantage of it.

'It's just a small problem,' she murmured, keeping her response deliberately vague. 'Nothing I can't handle.'

'You sure?'

She stood up, praying her legs would hold her. 'Positive.' He didn't believe her, she could tell. She wished he weren't so observant, or that she was better at dissembling. 'What are you doing here? Lisa said you wouldn't be in until tomorrow.'

'I had some files I needed to pick up. I also hoped to find you here.'

'Why?'

'So I could invite you to dinner.'

'Why?' she repeated, this time with a suspicious edge.

His eyes narrowed. 'Interesting answer. Most people respond to a dinner invitation with a polite yes or no.'

'We're not most people,' she pointed out. 'And after yesterday I'm sure you can understand my hesitation.'

He tossed his suit coat and briefcase on the chair in front of her desk. 'If you'd rather, we can wait until tomorrow and have our discussion here, at the office. Or we can go out, have a relaxing dinner and negotiate in private.' He folded his arms across his chest. 'Which would you prefer?'

With all that had happened today, she'd completely forgotten about Damien's ultimatum. A hysterical laugh bubbled up inside her. Such wonderful choices. She could sell her shares in Caldwell's and end up as the scapegoat for the leaks plaguing the company, or she could stay, try and find the real villain and suffer the consequences Damien threatened for not selling.

'Dinner would be fine, thanks.' To her horror, her voice broke. He took a quick step toward her, but she snatched up the phone, holding it to her chest like a shield. 'Let me make a quick phone call and I'll be ready.' To her relief, the betraying wobble vanished and she sounded almost normal.

'Sable, what——?'

'Not now!' She took a quick gulping breath. 'Please, Damien. Not now.'

She sensed that he wanted to argue, to force her to confide in him. But to her relief he didn't press her. With a reluctant nod, he returned to his office, presumably to get his files. She didn't waste any time in placing a call to Millie Trainer, Kyle's 'Nanna', to warn her of the change in plans. She also had a swift, one-sided conversation with Kyle. 'I'll see you when I get home.' Noisy smacking sounds blasted her through the earpiece and a smile broke free for the first time that day. 'I love you too, sweetheart. Bye.'

Just as she hung up, Damien returned. He crossed the room and dropped a handful of files into his leather case. 'I didn't realize I'd be ruining your plans for the evening when I invited you to dinner,' he commented.

How much of her conversation had he overheard? she wondered. Too much, judging from the black expression darkening his face. 'You aren't ruining my plans,' she said with amazing calm. 'You've just postponed them.'

His mouth tightened. 'I see.' He picked up his briefcase and slung his suit coat over his shoulder. 'Shall we go? I have a car waiting.'

She nodded in acknowledgement and led the way to the elevators. Standing at his side within the confining cubicle as they rode to the underground garage, she couldn't help but remember yesterday morning—remember how it had felt to have her back pressed tight against his broad chest, his warm breath stirring the curls at her temple, the slow, possessive stroke of his hand stealing up her hip as his fingers fanned intimately across her abdomen. She shivered. It seemed as if an eternity had passed since then.

A moment later the doors parted and he motioned her toward the sleek limousine idling a few steps away. 'When did you start using a driver?' she inquired with a saccharine-sweet smile, praying he wouldn't sense how disturbing she'd found those brief, intrusive memories.

He didn't take offense, as she expected. Instead he shot her an impatient glance. 'Can the wisecracks, Sable. You know I only use the car when I'm entertaining clients.' He opened the door before the chauffeur had a chance. 'Get in.'

She obeyed, sliding across the plush leather seats. 'Is that why you canceled our meeting today?' she asked, more abruptly than she'd intended. 'Because you were busy entertaining clients?'

He joined her, sitting far too close for comfort. He shot her a sharp glance and sudden understanding dawned in his eyes. 'It wasn't deliberate, Sable,' he said in a surprisingly gentle voice. 'This appointment came up without warning and I couldn't postpone it. Didn't Lisa tell you to call if you needed to speak to me?'

Sable stared out the window as they left the garage, his unexpected kindness more difficult to deal with than his animosity. 'She told me.' They turned onto Montgomery Street, working their way toward the bay. Rush-hour traffic had only eased slightly, making it slow going.

'Besides, I thought an extra day would give you time to think, to consider all your options.'

She rounded on him. 'You didn't leave me any options, in case you've forgotten.'

'I gave you two: to sell——'

'Or to suffer the consequences,' she cut in harshly.

His searching gaze settled on her face once again. 'What's wrong, Sable?' he murmured.

She stiffened. She didn't want his understanding, his consideration. She could stand up to his fury; she'd fall apart beneath his tenderness. 'You know what's wrong. You've put me in an untenable position. What do you expect? For me to act as though nothing's happened, that dinner tonight is a pleasant diversion?'

'No. But I do expect a certain level of professional behavior.'

That tore it! Her gaze flashed upward to lock with his. 'If this were a business predicament, I'd be thoroughly professional. But this isn't business. This is personal and you damned well know it. So I'm afraid you're stuck with a less than professional response.'

She regretted losing her temper the moment she saw Damien's reaction. He looked like a tiger that had just sprung from its cage.

'You want to drop the pretense, is that it? Fine,' he practically snarled. 'I'm happy to play hardball. But don't complain if it gets rough. Remember you asked for it.'

'I didn't ask for a thing!' The words burst from her. 'This whole situation is your idea, your decision. You want to hurt me and this is the means you've chosen to do it.'

'Hurt you?' A small, enigmatic smile touched his mouth. 'How is that possible? You have to care in order to be hurt.'

Before she could rally sufficiently to respond, the limousine eased to a stop and the driver opened the door. Stepping from the vehicle, Sable stiffened, realizing they'd arrived at a pier where a familiar-looking launch rocked against its mooring. She spun around. 'Where are we going?' she demanded.

'You know where.'

She paled. There were only two possibilities, neither one acceptable. 'Damien, no. Don't do this to me.'

He caught her arm and urged her toward the boat. 'I'm offering dinner, Sable, not torture. This will give us the privacy we need.'

'So will my office.' She stopped at the bottom of the ramp leading to the launch and turned to face him. 'Why don't we have this conversation tomorrow?'

He stood square in the center of the gangway, blocking her line of retreat. 'I explained that to you. I don't want anyone from Caldwell's overhearing our conversation.' He spoke in quiet, implacable terms. 'That means it's either Nikolai's or my place. Now, which will it be?'

The alternatives went from bad to worse. She glanced longingly at the limo. 'Once again, you leave me no choice.'

He didn't move. 'Which will it be?' he repeated.

She sighed. 'Nikolai's.'

'I thought as much.' He assisted her aboard. 'Inside the cabin or out?'

'Outside,' she decided. 'I don't often get the chance to enjoy the sun and sea air.'

She settled in the padded seat close to the bow. A moment later, they cast off. A stiff breeze caught at her hair, teasing the curls about her face into total disarray. But she didn't care. Despite the tension of the coming evening, she slowly unwound beneath the waning rays of the sinking sun. Off toward the entrance of the bay, ghostly tendrils of fog crept steadily across the water toward them, enshrouding most of the Golden Gate Bridge so that only the bright red peaks of the uppermost spans rose above the roiling mist.

'That's better.' Damien spoke from behind her.

She brushed a stray curl from her eyes and glanced back at him. 'What's better?'

'You're beginning to relax.'

'It's been a stressful day,' she confessed.

'I could tell. You looked like you'd shatter into a thousand pieces at the first wrong word.' Without warning, he removed his suit coat and dropped it around her shoulders.

It was such an intimate gesture, possessive, protective, strangely arousing. The warmth from his body still clung to the encompassing folds of the jacket and his cologne teased her senses. She shut her eyes to conceal the sudden rush of tears. 'I still might shatter,' she surprised herself by admitting. 'I'm feeling a bit delicate.' But how much of that feeling could be attributed to the events of that day and how much to Damien's presence she couldn't say.

'You want to talk about it?'

She shook her head, emotion closing her throat. 'It's nothing you can help with,' she told him in a husky voice. 'I have to take care of it on my own.' She sensed his withdrawal, but it couldn't be helped. How could she trust him to help when he'd made his desire for revenge so clear?

They didn't converse after that. Sable didn't mind. She enjoyed being on the sea again even if it was in the confines of the bay. She tipped her head back and watched the gulls dip and wheel overhead, relishing the rock and sway of the boat as it motored through the choppy waters. All too soon they approached the lights and bustle of the village of Sausalito. She adored the winding streets and specialty shops of the small, Mediterranean-style community. She and Damien had whiled away many an hour at some of the sidewalk cafés. The launch bypassed the center of town and continued further north, coming alongside the narrow pier by Nikolai's.

Nikolai himself came out to greet them, shaking hands with Damien and kissing Sable effusively on both cheeks. 'It is good to see you together again,' he declared in his deep, booming voice. He wrapped a beefy arm around her waist and guided her up the ramp to the restaurant. 'Come. Your table is ready. And dinner tonight... well, let me just say it will be a surprise and a delight.'

'It always is with you,' Damien commented.

'This is true. So tell me, Mr Hotshot Businessman, what have you done to my Sable?' Nikolai glanced over his shoulder and glared, while Sable watched on in amusement. It never ceased to amaze her, the latitude Damien allowed his friend. 'She looks like she carries the weight of the world on her shoulders. This is your fault, yes?'

'Some of it,' Damien conceded, with a humorous glint in his eyes. 'But I believe today's weight is all her own doing.'

'This is not good. I won't stand for it on your first time back to my restaurant in so long. Wait one minute.' Nikolai snapped his fingers. 'I have just the thing. Something that will make her forget all problems for the night.'

'*Her* is still here, in case you've forgotten,' Sable remarked drily. 'And I'm fine, thank you very much.'

'Fine? Hah! You make a good joke.' Nikolai threw open a side door that led into a private parlor overlooking the bay. 'Sit and relax. I will return with a small treat in a few minutes.'

The room he showed them to was one of two on the premises and might have graced any fine home. It was small and intimate, with a table set up in an alcove affording a gorgeous view of Richardson Bay and Angel Island. And further in the distance glittered the lights of San Franciso. Off to one side of the room, chairs and a love seat were grouped in a secluded semicircle around a fireplace. Instead of a fire, a huge dried-flower arrangement filled the grate, the refreshing aroma of eucalyptus teasing the senses.

Determined to postpone the discussion that she knew Damien was impatient to begin, Sable excused herself to go and freshen up. In the bathroom, she splashed cold water on her face and retouched her makeup, using a heavy hand with the blush. For reasons she couldn't explain, she also unpinned her hair, leaving the dark curls loose about her shoulders. Stepping back from the mirror, she nodded. It helped. She didn't appear nearly as drawn.

Returning to the private dining room, she found that Nikolai had brought two huge goblets filled with a green iced drink. Sections of tropical fruit, a paper umbrella and half a dozen tiny plastic monkeys festooned the rim in crazed abandon.

'What is it?' she questioned, eyeing the concoction suspiciously.

'It's called Nikolai's Nectar and he warned that he won't bring our dinner until you'd drained the glass.'

'Uh-oh. Have you tried it?'

He shook his head, his expression amused. 'I thought I'd wait for you.'

'Coward.' It took two hands just to lift the goblet. She took a quick sip from the straw and nearly choked. 'If I drain what's in this glass, I won't be able to eat any dinner because I'll have passed out,' she observed.

'I suspected as much. But a little won't hurt you.' He picked up his own glass and crossed to the love seat. 'Come and sit down and enjoy the view. Our discussion can wait a while.'

Until she'd consumed more of Nikolai's Nectar? she wondered in a rare moment of cynicism. Not likely. As soon as she figured out a safe place to dump it, half this drink would be plant fertilizer. Or would that kill the poor plant? She nibbled at her lower lip. She'd just have to risk it.

Instead of joining Damien on the love seat, she kicked off her pumps and curled up on the padded window seat near by. If she was to keep her head, she needed to stay as far from him as possible. She took another sip of her drink. And she needed to slow down her consumption of this green stuff. A huge potted philodendron stood within reach and she snuck out a finger to see if it was real.

'Don't bother,' Damien said. 'It's fake. You'll just have to drink it.'

'Is there anything that escapes your notice?' she complained, jerking her hand back.

'No, nothing.' He stood and walked toward her. His voice lowered, deepened. 'Your hair is on fire.'

She stared up at him, her breath catching in her throat. 'What?'

'The lights outside the window are red.' He reached out, his fingers brushing back the curls framing her face. 'They're caught in your hair, like hot embers licking at a nugget of coal.' He towered over her—large, indomitable and more attractive than any man had the right to be.

She closed her eyes to shut out the potent sight. 'Damien, don't,' she whispered, gripping the icy glass between her fingers. 'Not tonight. I can't bear it.'

'Look at me.' His thumb brushed her cheekbone and she trembled helplessly. 'Look at me,' he repeated. Slowly she lifted her gaze to his. He stared down at her, his green eyes darkening with unwavering resolve. 'It's too late to stop. We play this game to the bitter end. Fight me and you'll only make it more difficult for yourself.'

'Don't do this,' she pleaded. 'You'll regret it. I swear you will. Just let me go.'

He shook his head before she'd even finished speaking. 'I can't. I won't.'

She really hadn't expected any other response. She struggled to recover her composure. 'You...you said we didn't have to discuss business now,' she reminded him. 'Have you changed your mind?'

'No. We'll wait until after dinner as agreed,' he said. 'There's something else I'd rather discuss, anyway.'

She gazed at him apprehensively. 'What is it?'

A final glimmer of daylight caught the steely glitter of his eyes before dusk overtook the room, plunging his face into shadow. 'Who the hell is Kyle?' he demanded.

CHAPTER FIVE

PANIC set in and Sable shrank into the deepening shadows, hoping her expression wouldn't betray her. Thank heavens no one had bothered to switch on the lights. 'How do you know about Kyle?' Even to her own ears her voice sounded thready and nervous.

'Your phone conversation.'

'You listened?' She couldn't believe his nerve.

'Your voice carried,' he corrected her. 'Close the door next time you want privacy. Now, who is he?'

Sable lifted the glass to her lips and took a long, desperate swallow, stalling for time. 'That's none of your business,' she said at last.

'You're right. It's not. Is he your lover?'

'No!'

'He lives with you, doesn't he?'

'Yes!' She took a quick, steadying breath. 'I repeat, it's none of your business.'

'Who is he, Sable? You might as well tell me. Because if you don't I'll find someone who will.'

She stiffened. It wouldn't be too difficult to find that someone, either. Quite a few people at Caldwell's knew about Kyle. Eventually, Damien would find a chatty employee willing to talk about the son she'd given birth to a mere seven months after her marriage to Leonard. It was a small wonder he hadn't found out already. And once he did discover the truth it wouldn't take him long to put two and two together and figure out why she'd been so anxious to keep Kyle's existence a secret. After all, if he were Leonard's son, why the big mystery?

No, she didn't dare risk telling Damien anything. His anger at learning about the leaks five years ago would be nothing compared to his anger should he learn about Kyle. She licked her lips, tasting the fruity tang of her iced drink. With luck it would give her a bit of courage, because she needed every scrap she could muster—even the temporary kind courtesy of Nikolai's Nectar.

She lifted her glass, meeting his fierce gaze over the rim with a calm she was far from feeling. 'Kyle's a relative.'

His eyes narrowed. 'I thought you didn't have any relatives.'

'Well, you thought wrong.' Her voice sharpened. 'And I won't answer any more of your questions about him, so don't bother asking.'

A mocking smile tugged at the corner of his mouth. 'Good try...but wrong. You'll answer my questions. It's just a matter of when. Is he related to Caldwell?'

She glared at him, furious that he insisted on pursuing the conversation. 'This is ridiculous. Why do you care who he is? What if he is my lover? What is it to you?'

'Is he?' The question came, swift and clipped. 'Is that why you're being so secretive?'

'No! I just don't understand why you're persisting with this. You've been out of my life for five years now. Why the sudden interest in my personal affairs?'

'Affairs?'

She made an impatient gesture. 'You know what I mean. Why pursue this particular issue?'

He tilted his head to one side, watching her with a nerve-shredding intentness. 'Because something doesn't add up and I'm beginning to suspect that Kyle is part of it. Care to explain him to me now?'

'Not really.' She lost it then, unable to stand another minute of his probing. 'Stay out of it, Damien! I'm warning you, this is none of your business.'

He lifted an eyebrow. 'Are you threatening me?'

'No,' she quickly denied. 'As I said, I'm warning you.'

'Strange how your warnings sound so much like threats. I think... Yes.' He nodded in satisfaction. 'I think it was a threat. I must be getting close for you to try something so pointless, not to mention desperate.' His eyes narrowed. 'But I'm not quite as close as I intend to get, my sweet Sable. Not by a long shot.'

'Damien...' she whispered in distress. The air seemed thick and heavy, and she struggled to breathe, struggled to think of a way to call him off the chase, to quell his hunter's instinct. But nothing came to mind, and she sat without moving, mesmerized, held like a frightened deer by the predatory gleam in his bold green eyes.

To her intense relief, the door opened behind him and a waiter bearing a huge tray entered, followed by Nikolai. 'What? No lights?' He flicked a switch by the door and a soft, muted glow filled the room. 'This is better, yes?'

Damien ignored him, leaning closer to Sable. 'And just so you know,' he murmured. 'This discussion isn't over, just postponed.'

She fought her panic and anger, and summoned a tight smile. 'Don't count on it.'

He straightened and stepped back from the window seat. 'Oh, but I am counting on it. Your challenge has been met. Let the games begin.'

Nikolai approached, curtailing any further conversation. 'Ah, good,' he said, beaming in delight. 'You have finished your drink. You like?'

Sable stared down at her empty glass in dismay. Sure enough, only a cherry remained, swimming at the bottom in a puddle of melted ice. 'It was delicious,' she confessed.

'Yes. I agree,' Nikolai said without a trace of modesty. 'And dinner, it is even better. Come and sit. Joey! What do you wait for? The candles, you young fool. Light them. Our guests are hungry.'

Sable crossed to the table. Dinner at Nikolai's always came as a surprise. They were never permitted to order. Their meal consisted of whatever Nikolai felt like preparing that day. Never once had she found cause to complain and she suspected that tonight would prove no different. Damien held her chair while Joey lit the candles.

'And now, my most popular creation.' With a flourish Nikolai presented their appetizer. 'Oysters Alcatraz.'

Sable inhaled sharply, shooting a startled glance toward Damien. From the humor lightening his expression, the significance of being served the fabled aphrodisiac hadn't escaped him either. 'My favorite,' she claimed, practically choking on the words.

'The favorite of all lovers,' Nikolai boasted with brash aplomb. 'And, to celebrate your return to my establishment, I wish to treat you to a bottle of my finest champagne. The favored drink of lovers to go with the favored food. What could be better, huh?'

He positioned an ice bucket and stand at Damien's elbow and made short shrift of removing the wire and foil from the bottle. A moment later he poured the foaming champagne into flutes. Scrutinizing the table one final time, he gave a nod of satisfaction. 'Na zdorov'e!' he saluted them, and then he and Joey disappeared out the door.

'All the trappings of a romantic evening,' Sable murmured, attempting a smile. 'Little does he know.'

Damien speared an oyster, consuming it with obvious relish. 'Nikolai knows far more than you might think.'

That gave her pause. 'Such as?' she questioned, raising an eyebrow.

'That we're here to discuss business. Try an oyster. They're quite good.'

She picked up her fork and scooped a morsel from the shell, slipping it into her mouth. The meat was smooth and tender, and the asparagus young and crisp, with just the proper hint of anisette and a sinful amount of butter. He was right. They were perfectly delicious. 'If Nikolai knows it's a business dinner, then why...?' She gestured toward the oysters and champagne.

'He hopes we'll end up discussing more than just business.'

Oh, he did, did he? Well, not if she could help it. She lowered her gaze and applied herself to the oysters. The mere thought of renewing their conversation about Kyle caused her muscles to clench in dread.

To her relief, Damien kept the conversation casual, and Sable found herself relaxing. She even laughed at some of his stories. He had so many wonderful qualities and she'd fallen in love with each and every one of them—his strength, his passion, his brilliance. But most of all she loved those rare moments when he let down his guard, when he revealed the compassion and kindness that only a very strong man felt comfortable exposing.

They finished the last of the oysters and a companionable silence settled between them. 'How did this summer's picnic go?' she asked impulsively.

Hawke Enterprises sponsored a yearly picnic for handicapped and underprivileged children that kicked off the opening of their summer camp. Located in the mountains, far from the city, the camp was run by trained professionals and gave the children an opportunity to experience many of the activities they wouldn't otherwise be able to enjoy—horseback riding, canoeing, water sports... The list was endless. But most of all the counselors stressed teamwork and fought to instill self-respect and self-confidence in the children.

It was a charity that was dear to Sable's heart, one she'd continued to donate to even after she'd been fired, though she'd been careful to keep her contributions anonymous.

'The picnic went very well. We received a lot of media attention this year, which helped with donations. Enough came in to purchase the land for a second camp.'

'Really? That's wonderful! I... saw the segment they did on the news.' She peeked up at him, her dark eyes gleaming with barely suppressed laughter. 'Did you get ribbed about it?'

'For weeks.' He frowned, though she knew he wasn't really annoyed. 'Damned kid. Jerome. That was his name. He did it on purpose—waited until the camera focused on me before letting fly with that water balloon.'

Sable bit down on her lip to keep from laughing. 'Your expression was priceless. I think the newscaster really believed you were going to kill that poor boy.' She wrinkled her brow, struggling to remember. 'What did she say?'

'She didn't say anything—at first. She shrieked loud enough to be heard in three counties,' he said in disgust. 'Then she yelled, "Save the poor boy before that beast murders him!"'

'It only made her look foolish,' Sable said consolingly. 'I'm surprised they didn't dub it out.'

He shook his head in satisfaction. 'They couldn't. It was a live broadcast. And when it played so well with their viewers they repeated it intact.'

She chuckled. 'Much to the newswoman's chagrin, I'm sure.'

It had been an electric moment. The aloof businessman, water dripping from his hair and shoulders, faced off against a pint-sized devil bent on mischief. When Damien had snatched the youngster into the air, Sable had thought the newswoman would have a conniption. And then he'd pretended to slip, tumbling with Jerome into the shallow wading pool behind them, and the tension had been broken with hysterical laughter.

But the most poignant moment of all had been when Damien and the boy had surfaced, totally drenched and grinning with unmistakable male camaraderie. Jerome had thrown his arms around Damien's neck, clinging to him with such a look of adoration that it had brought tears to Sable's eyes. And Damien... He'd ruffled the boy's short, wiry hair, the most incredible look of tenderness creeping across his stern features.

Was that how he'd be with Kyle? she wondered wistfully. Would he show that same caring, allow his guard to drop sufficiently to let love, in the shape of a small, impish boy, wriggle in? A picture formed in her mind, a picture as precious as it was impossible and her breath caught in an audible gasp.

He instantly keyed in on her reaction. 'What's wrong?'

She dropped her gaze to hide her pain. 'A passing thought. A foolish thought.' And that was precisely what it was—foolish.

'Something you can share?'

She shook her head. 'I don't think so.'

'More secrets?' He leaned across the table, clasping her hand in his. 'One of these days they're going to catch up with you. What will you do then, Sable?'

She shrugged uneasily. 'I'll cross that bridge when I get to it, I guess. What else can I do?'

'You might try honesty for a change.'

She tilted her head to one side. 'That from a man bent on revenge?' She tugged her fingers from his grasp. 'I don't think so. But thanks for the suggestion.'

'I hope you don't regret it.'

'I hope not too,' she whispered.

But she already did. Unfortunately, regretting the choices she'd made five years ago could prove dangerous in the extreme, picturing Damien with Kyle even more so. Still, she couldn't help wondering if she'd made a horrible mistake, if she shouldn't have somehow forced a confrontation with Damien, told him about her pregnancy. But he'd been out of the country—beyond her reach. And she'd been afraid—afraid of what he might do to her and their child, afraid that he'd use her vulnerability to exact an unconscionable revenge. She'd also discovered in the past days that that fear, reasonable or not, hadn't diminished with time.

She glanced at him. He sipped his champagne, the candlelight highlighting the sweeping curve of his cheekbones and catching in the green of his eyes and the streaks of gold in his hair. She'd explored every inch of that face, knew it as intimately as her own. It was only his thoughts and emotions he kept so closely protected. Her mouth compressed. If she'd told him about her pregnancy, more than likely he wouldn't even have believed the baby was his. He'd as good as accused her of sleeping with Leonard at the same time she'd been with him. No, she'd made the right choice in keeping Kyle's existence a secret.

Their main course arrived then. To her delight Nikolai had prepared lobster thermador, her very favorite dish. 'Seems he's pulled out all the stops,' she murmured once the waiter had departed.

'Nikolai is a romantic,' Damien said. 'He wants everything perfect, hoping this will be the start of a second chance for us.'

'If that's what he's hoping, he's going to be sadly disappointed,' she said lightly. 'Though I'm surprised he knows so much about our private life.'

'Private? Hardly. Your defection was quite public,' he stated coolly.

'And you've never forgiven me for that, have you?' She selected a rosy cube of lobster dripping with sauce and Swiss cheese. It practically melted in her mouth.

'Forgiven?' he questioned harshly. 'No. Nor have I ever understood it.'

Her fork crashed to the table. 'You never understood because you wouldn't accept any of my explanations!'

'You mean your lies?' he bit out.

'They weren't lies. Oh, this is ridiculous!' She clenched her hands, her voice tight with fury. 'You preferred to believe that I'd lie and cheat, that I'd actually steal from you, rather than see the truth. You even dared to suggest that I could conduct an ardent affair with you while taking another man to bed on the side. Have you any idea what that did to me, knowing how little you trusted me, Damien?'

His expression frosted over, his eyes flashing a warning. 'The proof was incontrovertible.'

'Only to a closed mind,' she insisted. 'You were looking for an excuse to doubt me and I want to know why.'

He picked up his champagne flute, swirling the contents so that tiny bubbles shimmered in the depths of the pale gold wine. 'You're imagining things.'

'Am I?' Suddenly it seemed quite clear. The fact that he'd never completely let down his guard with her, but had always kept a small part of himself aloof and distant, became oddly significant. 'Am I imagining it, Damien?' she asked intently.

He returned her gaze and she'd never seen him more remote, more withdrawn. 'Don't try and dump this in my lap. Right after I fired you, you accepted a job from Caldwell. What else was I to believe?'

'I had no choice!' she insisted sharply. 'I had bills to pay!'

A muscle leapt in his jaw. 'That's a load of crock and you know it. Selling those bids to Caldwell's should have made you a wealthy woman.' His mouth twisted. 'Of course, marrying Caldwell made you even wealthier.'

Every scrap of color drained from her face. 'I won't discuss my marriage with you. It's absolutely none of your business. But I will say this.' She leaned forward to emphasize her point, her voice trembling with the strength of her passion. 'If I'd sold information to Caldwell's as you claimed, I wouldn't have had to work— money wouldn't have been an issue. But what about if I didn't sell you out? What if I didn't lie? Did you ever consider that?'

He didn't relent. 'I considered it. Until you proved me wrong.'

'I keep telling you—it was all a horrible mistake!'

'Then why work for the man?' he demanded, animosity breaking through his rigid control. 'It damned you in everyone's eyes. Even you must realize that.'

'I realize it. Dear lord, I've *lived* with that knowledge hanging over my head every day of the past five years,' she cried. 'But I had bills to meet, a rent to pay, food to buy. And no one would hire me...except Caldwell. I turned him down the first two times he asked, insulted that he'd think I'd work for a company capable of such duplicity. But as the weeks passed my pride wasn't as important as earning a living, putting food on the table. So I accepted his third offer and thanked heaven for his persistence.'

'Why was he willing to hire you?'

'Maybe because I'm good at my job.' Her gaze, angry and defiant, locked with his, condemning him for his relentless suspicion. 'Or maybe he hired me because he knew the truth—knew exactly how his company got hold of that bid information, knew that I never deliberately betrayed you. Perhaps he even felt guilty.'

Damien grew still, his head cocked to one side, and for the first time Sable thought she might have struck a chord with him. 'So why marry him?'

His question dashed all hope. 'He asked.' The answer was flippant and did nothing to redeem her. But she didn't care, couldn't care. What else could she possibly say? That she'd married Leonard because she was pregnant and adrift, and more frightened than she'd ever been in her life?

His eyes narrowed, cynicism tainting his expression. 'Interesting how thorough your explanations have been. Until now, that is. Until you have to try and justify why you married a man old enough to be your father.'

The fight drained from her. She couldn't win this battle; she'd been foolish even to think it possible. Dropping her gaze, she applied herself to the lobster. 'You forgot to mention,' she murmured drily, 'that Leonard was old enough to be my father *and* stinking rich.'

He released an exasperated sigh. 'Your humor is out of place.'

She could either laugh or she could cry. But she sensed that once the tears came she'd be unable to stop them. She forced a shaky smile to her lips. 'Right now,' she admitted with devastating candor, 'a sense of humor is all I have left.'

Annoyance flashed in his eyes for a fleeting moment, but whether it was directed at her or himself she couldn't tell. 'Then eat,' he directed briskly. 'Just let me know when you're ready to do battle again.'

She did as he suggested, enjoying the rare treat of a dinner out. It wasn't until they were sipping the last of the champagne that he resumed their discussion. 'Have you reached a decision about selling your Caldwell shares?'

'Back to business?' she asked with notable reluctance.

'Afraid so.'

'I... I'm willing to sell,' she confessed. 'But I'd like time.'

He inclined his head. 'How much time?'

'I'm not sure.' Replete, she pushed her plate aside. 'The end of the month should be sufficient, I guess.' That gave her until Ryan submitted his final report to complete her inquiries. If she hadn't found out who'd leaked the information to A.J. Construction by then, it wouldn't matter how much time Damien allowed. She'd be cast in the role of head scapegoat and that would be the end of it.

'Why do you need time? What are you hoping to accomplish in the next three weeks that could change anything?'

How could she possibly answer that without revealing what she'd learned from Alex Johnson? What excuse could she use? She bit down on her lip. 'I——'

'Does your hesitation have something to do with what happened at Caldwell's today?' he cut in abruptly.

'Excuse me?'

'You heard me. That phone call I walked in on before we left the office. Did it have anything to do with losing Luther's development project?'

'Why would you think that?'

'You're dancing around your answers again. Talk to me straight for once,' he ordered, irritation clear in his voice. 'You were upset—more than upset—by that call.'

'That's none——'

He tossed his linen napkin on to the table. 'Don't say it. Not again. Because unless that call was personal it's very much my business. I won't have you keeping secrets from me, not ones that affect Caldwell's.'

She hated deceiving him, hated the role she was forced to play. 'It was personal,' she claimed.

'You're lying,' he snapped. 'You're lying and I know it.'

She stiffened. 'How?'

He laughed, the sound incredibly weary. 'Sometimes your face is so open and clear, it reflects your every thought. Your eyes grow soft, like a rich black mist. And other times the light fades from your eyes and there's nothing there, no thought, no emotion, just this...murky emptiness. And that's when I know you're lying.'

She lowered her gaze, appalled that her most intimate thoughts and feelings were so easily read by him. 'Please, Damien. I'd rather not discuss that particular phone call.'

'Then let's discuss Luther. This entire situation reeks of a conspiracy. Why not admit it?'

He was taunting her deliberately, she could tell. He wanted to assess her reaction. She looked at him, suppressing her fear, forcing herself to deal with the problem with calm resourcefulness. 'You suspect there's been a leak, don't you?' she asked, cutting to the bottom line.

'You're damned right I do. I've spent the past twenty-four hours looking into it. And I've discovered that this isn't the only account we've lost. There have been four others in the past year. An interesting pattern, wouldn't you say?'

That did take her by surprise. 'So many? I had no idea. Do you really think those others had information leaked too?'

'Too?' he questioned sharply, her comment clearly condemning her. 'So you *do* think A.J. Construction had inside information on the Luther project.'

She sighed in defeat. She shouldn't have had quite so much of Nikolai's Nectar. She certainly shouldn't have followed it with several glasses of champagne, not when she needed to keep her wits about her in order to deal with Damien. 'Ryan's looking into the possibility. At least, he is with Luther.' Her brows drew together. 'It worries me, though, that you think they're all connected.'

'It should worry you more that I think you might be responsible,' he retorted.

Her mouth tightened. 'Is that what you plan? To blame me like last time?'

'Ah, but you were guilty last time.'

She pushed back her chair and stood up, crossing to the window. Lights from numerous boats twinkled out on the bay, though fog concealed most of the view. 'I'd like to leave,' she stated quietly, wrapping her arms around her waist.

His reflection appeared just behind her. 'Running away, Sable?'

'I prefer to call it a temporary retreat. I'm tired and need time to regroup.' She swung around. 'I want you to think about something, though. If I leaked that information, what possible motivation could I have?'

'I don't know,' he conceded slowly. 'But then, it took me a while to figure out your motivation before.' He dropped his hands on her shoulders, drawing her close. 'You'd better not be responsible for the leak. Because this time I won't hesitate to press charges. And then you won't have to worry about selling me your shares: you'll lose them to me.'

She didn't fight him as she should. Exhaustion gripped her and she relaxed against him, resting her head in the crook of his shoulder. Just for a minute she'd close her eyes and pretend that his hold was an embrace, his intent to comfort rather than accuse.

'You'd better not be responsible for the leak.' His words rang in her ears. She had so little time left to uncover the actual villain and vindicate herself. Unfortunately, she couldn't expect any help from Damien. Tears pricked her eyes. 'Maybe I should just sell out now.'

'You can. But I'll put a clause in the sales agreement. If you're guilty, the deal's off.'

She glanced up at him. 'Then I'll have to find the real culprit, won't I?'

He cupped her cheek, his thumb brushing her jaw. 'Are you sure she isn't right here?'

'Positive,' she said without hesitation.

He didn't argue, though she suspected he didn't quite believe her. 'Time will tell,' was all he said. 'Are you ready to go?'

She nodded. 'There's just one last thing I'd like to ask before we leave.' She licked her lips, steeling herself for this final battle. 'I . . . I have a request.'

Laughter lightened his eyes, the green as bright and vivid as newly unfurled leaves. 'Why doesn't that surprise me?'

'It's about your other . . . condition.'

He didn't pretend to misunderstand. 'About our sleeping together?'

She nodded. 'Were you serious about that?'

'Very.'

'Why?' The question burst from her before she could stop it. 'How could you insist on such a thing?'

His expression darkened, desire slipping across his face, heating his eyes and hardening his body. 'Because you're a temptation I can't resist. You're like a pool of water in the midst of a scorching desert. And I've been lost in that desert for five long years. I have to taste you, slip inside you, see if you feel as good as I remember or if it's all an empty mirage.'

'But not this way,' she argued desperately. 'Not with threats and coercion. Not with such cold-blooded deliberation.'

His laugh had a wry, husky quality to it. 'There's nothing cold-blooded about the way I feel.'

'You'll regret it, I swear you will,' she tried again.

He shrugged. 'Then I'll regret it.' His fingers slipped beneath the heavy fall of her hair, thrusting into the thick curls at the base of her neck. 'What's your request?'

Nervous dread balled in the pit of her stomach. 'If you insist on holding me to this . . . this *stipulation*, then I want to be the one to decide when and where.'

He inclined his head. 'Agreed.'

'No!' she cried recklessly. 'There is no agreement. There's only your demand and my submission. That certainly doesn't constitute an agreement.'

'It doesn't matter what you call it.' His arms tightened around her, fitting them together like two interlocking pieces, neither one complete without the other. 'This is what it's all about. The warmth of my hand against your breast, the stirring of our bodies when they touch. Our lips meeting, tasting.' His voice deepened. 'The feel of your body beneath mine, open and eager.'

Heat flashed through her, burning with an unmistakable urgency. 'But it's not love!' she protested, battling against the primitive hunger sweeping through her like wildfire.

Amusement flickered in his eyes. 'I never said it was. Call it love or concede it's lust. Whichever it is, I intend to enjoy it. And so will you, no matter how much you try and deny it.'

'No!' She shook her head, wishing she could refute his words, struggling to resist what was fast becoming more and more irresistible.

He didn't permit any further opposition, his method of silencing her immediate and effective. He lowered his head and kissed her. She murmured in dissent, but his mouth absorbed the distressed sound. He didn't force her; he didn't need to. Instead he reminded her of the intense delight to be found within his arms, seducing her with slow, deep kisses, teasing kisses, soul-wrenching kisses.

Reality deserted her, leaving her careening out of control. He was the sun, coaxing her toward his brilliant fire. She surrendered to his pull, spinning where he willed, bathed in his golden heat. Her heart had never truly belonged to her, she realized then. It had always rested within his care, his to cherish or destroy.

His mouth slid from hers and she gasped for breath, fought for sanity. 'You can't do this to me again. I won't let you!'

'You can't stop it. You're mine, body and soul. You've always been mine.' His hand caressed her hip and her response came as surely and naturally as a wave to the shore. 'You see? Deny it all you want; it doesn't alter a thing.'

She bowed her head. 'You won't change your mind?' she whispered.

'I can't. I won't.'

She lifted her head, tears trembling on the end of her lashes. 'Then heaven forgive you, because I never will.' And with that she ripped free of his arms and ran for the door. She had to get away, she had to leave *now* before she lost all control. Flinging it open, she threw an anguished glance over her shoulder, her expression filled with accusation and hopeless desire. And then she plunged into the fog-filled night.

CHAPTER SIX

'SABLE! Sable, stop!'

She heard Damien's footsteps pounding on the deck outside the restaurant, giving chase—and gaining on her. She ran recklessly onward, intent on escape, the breath sobbing in her throat, tears blinding her path. She'd always known that it would come to this, both of them reverting to their baser instincts—she the prey, fleeing before the predator, Damien giving chase, moving with cat-like speed, running her down to earth. Her heel caught on an uneven plank and just as she pitched forward his hands closed on her shoulders, saving her from a nasty fall.

'What the *hell* do you think you're doing?' he demanded, spinning her round to face him.

She tore free of his hold. 'Take your hands off me! I'm going home. Alone.' She swept her hair back from her eyes and glared at him with all the defiance she could muster, refusing to shrink from his wrath. To her confusion, he didn't look angry as much as concerned.

'You want to go home? Fine. I'll take you there.'

She shook her head stubbornly, trembling with emotion, struggling to catch her breath. 'I said alone. I'll...I'll catch a cab. Or take the ferry.'

He stepped between her and the walkway toward Sausalito. 'Not a chance. You came with me, you leave with me.'

'No! I'll——'

'Forget it, Sable.' His tone brooked no opposition and he shifted closer, as though in anticipation of her bolting again. 'You're not going home alone. I'll escort you to the launch. You can wait for me there while I settle up inside.'

She drew in a deep, shaky breath. She'd overreacted, she realized, allowed him to get to her, to break through her defenses. She'd panicked when she most needed to keep a level head. But it was all too much. Every time she turned around she faced a new battle—a battle she had no chance of winning.

Slowly she nodded, her rebellion draining away, to be replaced by an oppressive weariness. 'All right,' she said in a cool, remote voice. 'You may take me home.'

'Thank you.' Irony colored his words.

'No more, Damien,' she said, with a tiny sigh. 'Please. I've had enough.'

He apparently concurred. Wrapping a protective arm around her waist, he guided her down the ramp to the dock. 'Wait here,' he ordered, then stilled. Tucking a lock of hair behind her ear, he tilted her face toward the lights ringing the restaurant, his brows drawing together in a fierce frown. His thumb feathered across her cheek, tracing the path of her tears. 'You're exhausted.' He sounded almost apologetic. 'I should have realized.'

She didn't trust his compassion. It was just one more weapon in his arsenal, the latest attempt to slip beneath her guard. 'I'll be fine again tomorrow.' She had to be. There wasn't any other choice, not with the clock ticking steadily toward her doom. She had to act, not rest.

He helped her aboard. 'I'll be right back. Don't disappear on me.'

'I won't,' she murmured, and collapsed on the padded seat in the bow. She didn't have the energy to find her own way home, anyway. She certainly didn't have the energy to indulge in another chase. And that was precisely what would happen should she run. Damien would come after her again, and what might happen should he be forced to catch her a second time didn't bear consideration.

She stared out at the boats moored at a nearby yacht club. Sounds drifted across the water to her—the slap of waves against fiberglass hulls, the groan of wood dipping and swaying atop the choppy crests, the distant clang of a buoy marker. She found it oddly soothing and she relaxed against the seat cushions, taking a deep breath of rich, salty air.

Dinner with Damien had been a bad idea. A very bad idea. It had brought back too many memories, left her far too vulnerable. From now on she had to keep their relationship strictly professional. She couldn't allow herself to fall into the trap of thinking there could be anything more than Caldwell's between them—certainly not the love affair they'd once experienced. That path led to disaster. And she had too much at risk even to consider anything so insane.

Damien returned to the launch then, her purse beneath his arm. She couldn't believe she'd left it behind. She really must be losing her grip. He joined her in the bow, sitting much too close. But since she could hardly shift her position without subjecting herself to more of his caustic remarks she stayed put.

'You sure you don't want to go inside the cabin?' he asked. 'There's quite a breeze.'

She shook her head and he didn't attempt to change her mind. Instead he draped his jacket about her shoulders, just as he had on their trip over. A few minutes later they cast off, motoring out into the bay. Fog cocooned them, ebbing and flowing about the boat and dusting Sable's hair with diamond-like droplets of dew. It was as though they existed in their own little world, just the two of them. In the distance a fog horn broke the silence, the sound muffled, its mournful cry an accurate reflection of her own despondency. She closed her eyes, totally drained, the rocking of the boat, the throb of the engines lulling her toward a peaceful oblivion.

She stirred just as they docked, the launch bumping gently against the pier startling her awake. Good heavens, how could she have fallen asleep? It seemed incredible. She stiffened, realizing then that Damien held her. She must have turned into his embrace as she slept for he supported her securely, her head cushioned against his shoulder, his arms wrapped firmly about her waist. How many times during their years together had she drifted off in this very position? And how many times in the past five years had she awakened in the middle of the night, her arms empty and aching, her pillow damp with tears? Too many. She drew away, murmuring a flustered apology.

He made no comment, simply helped her to her feet, his hand beneath her elbow as she fought for balance on the lurching deck. 'I had the captain call ahead. The car should be waiting.'

'What time is it?' she asked, slipping his jacket from around her shoulders and handing it to him.

'Around midnight.'

'So late?'

He shrugged, not in the least concerned. 'We were at Nikolai's for quite some time. We had a lot to discuss, if you remember, a lot to settle.'

Not that they had managed to settle their differences, she realized uneasily. If anything, their positions were more adversarial than ever. She walked with Damien to the limo, giving the driver her Pacific Heights address before getting in.

'I thought Caldwell had an estate in St Francis Woods,' Damien said as the car pulled away from the pier. 'What was it called? Rat's Nest?'

'Fox's Lair. And you don't need to sound so sarcastic. Your place in Sausalito isn't exactly shabby.'

'So, what happened to the Lair?' he questioned.

'Leonard sold it,' she replied, hoping the brevity of her response would put an end to his questions.

It didn't.

'Why?' he persisted.

She glanced at him, something in his tone arousing her suspicions. Why the questions? What did he want now? But the shadows that cut across his face defeated her attempts to decipher his expression. 'He sold it trying to save the design firm.'

'A pointless gesture.'

She laughed shortly. 'You should know. You're the reason the firm went bankrupt.'

'Wrong,' came the biting retort. 'Lenny was the reason the firm went bankrupt. I merely took advantage of his bad business decisions. If it hadn't been me cleaning up after him, it would have been someone else.'

She turned to look out the window. 'My mistake.'

'You don't believe me, do you?'

She faced him again, holding on to her temper through sheer grit and determination. 'I believe you did everything within your power to break Leonard. And you succeeded. I also think there's no point in discussing this further.' For once luck was with her and they pulled to a stop on the steep slope outside her house, putting an end to the discussion. 'Thank you for dinner. Goodnight.'

He caught her hand before she could open the door. 'Let me tell you something. It didn't take much effort to bring Leonard down. I could have sat back and done nothing and he'd still have ended up losing everything. All I did was expedite the inevitable.'

'Why, how charitable of you, Damien. I'm sure my husband appreciated that,' she said with undisguised contempt. 'Now let me go!'

He actually had the audacity to laugh. 'Not a chance.'

Anger barbed her voice, her words coming fast and furious. 'Oh, but you will. Once your conditions are met, you'll be out of my life. And this time it'll be for good. I'm not Leonard. You may take Caldwell's from me, but you won't destroy me like you did him. I won't let you.'

'No, you won't, will you? You'll fight me every step of the way, bending when necessary, but never breaking.' His hand cupped her cheek. 'Well, fight all you want, my love, but it won't make any difference. You belong to me. You always have. It's time you faced that fact.'

The breath hissed from her lungs. 'That changed five years ago, Damien. What we had is gone.'

'I wish it were,' he told her roughly. 'Otherwise I wouldn't want to do this every time you come near.'

Not giving her time to react, he lowered his head and took her mouth, took without mercy or hesitation. He drove his hands deep into her hair, holding her close. It was exquisite, a rapture that swept away all knowledge of right or wrong, all awareness of propriety. It was raw and elemental and powerful and she clutched at his shirt, opening to him, the need to respond an instinct she found impossible to withstand.

'You see?' he muttered against her lips. 'It's still there, in every word you utter, every look you give, every touch we exchange. We're connected. You're mine, Sable. Deny it all you want, but it won't change the truth.'

'No! No, you're wrong.' With a tiny cry of distress she grabbed the door handle and scrambled from the limousine, intent on escaping to the safety of her house. Before she could, however, Damien stepped from the car.

'Sable...'

Reluctantly, she turned around. 'What is it now?' she demanded.

He held out her purse. 'I thought you might want this.' He paused, a hint of a smile playing about his mouth. 'Otherwise I might be forced to come in and return it to you. And I suspect you'd rather that didn't happen. Or am I mistaken?'

He wasn't mistaken and they both knew it. Without a word, she snatched the purse from his hand and hurried up the stairs to her door. She was running away again— an act guaranteed to catch the interest of a hungry predator. Once she'd reached the relative security of her porch, she risked a quick glance over her shoulder. Damien stood, leaning negligently against the door of the limo. But it was the expression on his face that followed her inside, followed her to the privacy of her bed and into the depths of her dreams....

It was the intent, savage expression of a lion about to pounce.

* * *

Damien appeared at the connecting door to Sable's office first thing the next morning. 'Got a minute?' he asked, his demeanor thoroughly businesslike.

'Sure,' she replied a trifle warily, tucking Ryan's latest missive out of sight. Not that it revealed anything vital— just more possible names. More *impossible* names.

Meeting Damien's aloof gaze, she realized that last night might never have been. Not a hint of emotion disturbed the calm tenor of his voice, or touched the cool green of his eyes. She shouldn't allow his remoteness to throw her; certainly it hadn't all the years she'd worked for him. Separating business from their personal life had been as easy as slipping on and off a pair of shoes. Back then she'd bathed in the warmth of his love, secure that nothing could ever harm their relationship.

Or so she'd thought.

'I want you to clear your schedule in the mornings for the rest of the week,' he informed her.

She lifted her brows in surprise. 'Why?'

He tapped the papers in his hands. 'We have two vital contracts coming up for bid and I want us to work together on them—make sure we have all our bases covered.'

In other words, he wanted her working with him where he could keep an eye on her. She didn't air her suspicions, but nodded agreeably. 'Which contracts are these?'

'A shopping mall in Concord and a state-of-the-art computer complex for Dreyfus Industry.'

She sat back in her chair, impressed. 'Those are huge. Can we handle them?'

'Not alone. I'm going to pull my construction company in on this too.'

She titled her head to one side, her eyes narrowing in thought. 'What are you up to, Damien? Are you thinking about a merger, by any chance? Hawke absorbing Caldwell's?'

A strange smile crept across his mouth, further arousing her suspicions. 'Not at all,' he claimed. 'There's no advantage in consolidating the two firms. But there's a big advantage to pooling our resources on occasion.'

'And this is one of those occasions?'

'I think so.' He crossed to her desk, edging a hip on the corner closest to her. 'As long as we're discussing this, there's something else we'd better address.'

What now? she couldn't help but wonder. 'Yes?'

'I want to throw a reception the end of next week and hold it here. Doesn't the twentieth floor have facilities for occasions like that? A ballroom or something?' At her nod, he continued. 'Since the top management at Caldwell's has changed, I think it's important to have a friendly get-together with our key employees and principal clientele.'

'I see.' She tapped her blotter with the end of her pencil, the only outward sign of her annoyance. 'And you want me to make the arrangements, is that it?'

His smile was devastating. 'You were always good at it, Sable.'

'I still am,' she informed him coldly. 'But there's no point in playing games. Why not admit your plan right up front? You want me to throw the reception and introduce you around in order to make it clear to Caldwell staff—as well as to our clients—that you're in charge.'

His smile faded. 'Very astute. But don't look so offended. You've already agreed to sell your shares of Caldwell's to me. It's not like I'm taking anything away from you. Consider throwing this party a small statement of intent on your part—a guarantee, if you will. Our employees aren't stupid; nor are our clients. They'll read between the lines.'

'Read that I'm out and you're in?' He inclined his head in agreement and she asked, 'So, what's the rush? Why not wait a few weeks?'

His expression grew cold and hard. 'Someone is leaking information. You know it and I know it. You say you're innocent. If that's true, then someone else out there is responsible. I want to make it clear that they aren't dealing with an easy mark any more. They're dealing with me. And I don't take this sort of thing lying down.'

'An easy mark!' She straightened in her chair as she absorbed the insult. 'You must be joking.'

He didn't back down. 'Assuming you're innocent, that's precisely what you've been. This situation should have been caught and stopped months ago. And you damned well know it.'

'I wasn't in a position to stop it,' she protested. Not while Patricia ran the company.

'You still aren't.' He covered her hand with his, stopping the agitated rapping of her pencil. 'Now, will you organize the reception, or shall I handle it?'

She yanked her fingers from beneath his and tossed the pencil on to her blotter. 'I'll take care of it.'

'Fine. Lute has coffee ready. Shall we get started on those bids?'

Her mouth compressed. 'Of course,' she said, and stood, sweeping her papers together. 'Give me a minute to speak to Janine. I'll have her begin the preliminary arrangements for your reception and be right with you.' But she didn't like the idea of this party. Not one little bit. Unfortunately, however, she didn't have much choice in the matter.

The next week flew by. Between working with Damien, pulling together the information necessary to submit the bids, and going over preparations for the reception with Janine, she scarcely had time to catch her breath.

'Wait a minute,' Sable called to her secretary one afternoon, releasing an exasperated sigh. 'I've given you the wrong stack. These are the menus; you have the reports for Dreyfus. If I let that data out of my sight, Damien will have my head on a platter.'

With an understanding smile, her secretary traded papers. 'I thought those figures looked a little high for stuffed artichoke hearts.'

'Hmm. I'm not so sure. They seem darned close to me. How many refusals have you gotten for the reception?'

'Only one,' Janine admitted in surprise. 'Seems everyone's at a loose end this Friday.'

'More likely they've arranged to be at a loose end,' she said with a dry laugh. 'I think they find the whole situation too intriguing to pass up.' Janine hesitated, clutching the papers to her chest, and Sable lifted an eyebrow in question. 'Is there something else?'

'I was just wondering... Are you planning to leave the company, Mrs Caldwell?'

The question wasn't entirely unexpected, not considering the secretary's familiarity with her past—and Damien's. 'I'm thinking about it,' Sable admitted.

Unflattering color mottled Janine's cheeks. 'But what about Mr Caldwell?' she questioned tightly. 'It's an insult to his memory, turning his company over to that man.'

Sable trained her dark gaze on the older woman. 'I assume by "that man" you're referring to Mr Hawke,' she said gently. 'In case you've forgotten, he owns the majority of shares in this company, something he acquired without any help from me. If it makes you feel any better, Damien has no intention of dismantling the company or changing the name—at least, not as far as I know. With luck, the name will live on, even if there are no Caldwells actively running the business.'

Janine lowered her eyes. 'Yes, Mrs Caldwell. You're right, of course.'

Deliberately changing the subject, Sable said, 'If you'd call the caterers with those final changes, I'd appreciate it. And check with the florists about the centerpieces. They seemed rather iffy about the delivery time.'

'I'll get right on it,' Janine promised, making a final notation on her pad. 'Is there anything else?'

Sable sighed. 'A thousand things, I'm sure. But none you have to worry about right now. Thanks for your help on this one. I couldn't have done it without you.'

Janine nodded abruptly. 'It's my job.'

The door shut behind the secretary and Sable leaned back in her chair, closing her eyes. How many other employees felt as Janine did? she wondered with regret. Did they all believe she and Patricia had betrayed Leonard's memory? Though she agreed that it was a shame there weren't any Caldwells left to run the company, she didn't entirely blame Damien for that. Leonard and Patricia had to accept their fair share of the responsibility, too. Damien couldn't have bought his way into the company if Patricia hadn't sold out. Nor could he have driven them to the brink of bankruptcy if Leonard hadn't been such a poor businessman. Still... Caldwell's without a Caldwell. It was sad.

The next two days slid by as rapidly as the previous week. Sable stayed in constant touch with Ryan

Matheson, hoping against hope that they'd find something of significance before his report was due. But with only ten days remaining neither of them had been able to uncover how the bid information had been obtained or who might be responsible. Though after her discussion with Alex Johnson Sable had her suspicions. Now all she had to do was figure out a way to prove those suspicions.

To her relief there were also no further leaks, but she felt as though she stood on the edge of a towering cliff waiting... waiting for a storm hanging just offshore to break, waiting for the gale-force winds to sweep down from the heavens and hurl her over the edge into the abyss below. Her fate seemed inevitable, the only question... *when*.

Friday dawned bright and clear and Sable packed a garment bag to take to work. She doubted she'd have time to go home and get ready before the reception. Between double-checking the final arrangements for that night and tying up loose ends with Dreyfus before the weekend, it seemed the wisest course to bring a suitable dress with her and change at work.

Promptly at five that afternoon, the door between her office and Damien's opened, and he glanced in. 'I'm heading down to the gym for a quick workout and shower. I'll stop by in an hour so we can go to the reception together.'

'That's fine,' Sable said with a nod. 'I have a few odds and ends to finish up and then I'll change.'

'OK. One hour.' And with that he disappeared.

Twenty minutes later she threw down her pen and stretched. Lord, she was exhausted. She couldn't wait until tonight was behind her. She wasn't looking forward to the knowing glances and derisive comments hidden

behind artificial smiles. Though, after five years, she
should be used to it.

Shoving her papers to one side, she crossed to the
bathroom. She took her time, brushing out her hair and
piling it on top of her head in a formal knot. Next came
makeup, just a bit more dramatic than she normally
wore. Thank goodness women could hide behind such
a colorful and distracting facade. She needed every advantage she could get. Tilting her head to one side, she
nodded, satisfied with the results. Her dark eyes were
bright and clear, her coloring healthy and, though her
smile might be a bit fixed, with luck, no one would
notice.

Next she stripped off her suit and, unzipping the
garment bag, removed fresh underclothes and the
cocktail dress she'd decided to wear. She'd bought it
before Leonard's death and had never had the opportunity to wear it. A brilliant red, it made the perfect
statement—bold, undaunted and elegant.

She slipped on the dress, pleased with the fit. It molded
her figure, cupping her breasts and hugging her waist.
Circling the dress at the hips, layers of filmy scarves had
been cleverly and unobtrusively attached. As light as air,
they fell like the petals of a flower to just below her
knees. When she stood perfectly still they lay flat, a soft
and supple skirt. But the moment she stirred, the bright
red scarves shifted with a life of their own, billowing
and swaying as though to some secret music.

Slipping on heels the same flame-red color as her dress,
she dabbed a touch of perfume at her pulse-points, and
checked the mirror one final time. She hesitated, lifting
a hand to the base of her throat, and then reluctantly
crossed to the garment bag, removing a velvet box.

Flipping it open, she stared down at the ruby-and diamond-studded choker and earrings—Damien's last present to her. Aside from her wedding rings, it was the only expensive jewelry she'd kept. When Leonard's businesses had started to go downhill, she'd insisted that he sell the few pieces he'd given her.

Well, if Damien could wear her Rolex, she could wear his necklace and earrings. Not giving herself time to reconsider, she removed the jewelry from the satin bed and put them on. The gemstones flashed against her skin like bright red danger beacons. Trouble ahead, they seemed to warn. It was a warning she was forced to ignore.

Returning to the office, she discovered Janine delivering a final stack of mail. 'Anything urgent?' Sable asked, glancing at the pile.

'No, nothing.' Shoving gray-streaked bangs from her face, Janine frowned down at the desk. 'Now how did that get mixed in with your mail? This isn't addressed to you.' She reached into the pile and plucked out a large manila envelope. Across the upper left-hand corner, in huge block letters, was written 'A.J. Construction'. 'This goes to Mr Hawke. I'll just drop it on his desk on my way out.'

Sable licked her lips, staring at the envelope in her secretary's hand. Oh, no. This couldn't be good. Why in the world would Alex be contacting Damien? It could only mean one thing. She bit down on her lip. That storm swept ever closer to her precarious stance on the cliff. 'You're going down to the reception, Janine?' she managed to ask, praying her voice wouldn't reveal her agitation.

'Yes, Mrs Caldwell. I want to make sure the caterers are ready to go and give everything a final check.'

'Fine.' Sable forced her gaze away from the envelope. 'Thank you.'

Janine smiled. 'My pleasure.' She crossed to the connecting door that led to Damien's office and rapped lightly. Not receiving an answer, she walked in. A minute later she reappeared, empty-handed. 'Is there anything you need before I go?'

Sable shook her head, not daring to trust her voice again. She waited a full five seconds after Janine left before crossing to Damien's office. She hesitated in the doorway, debating the ethics of what she intended. But she had to get a look at that envelope. She had to get a look *in* that envelope. Slowly, she pushed the door wide and crossed the threshold. Her heart pounded and her breath came in quick, shallow gasps. She'd never done anything remotely like this before. If she was caught . . .

She glanced quickly over her shoulder as though expecting to find Damien lurking in the shadows, ready to leap out at her from behind the potted palms. This was ridiculous. The longer she delayed, the greater the likelihood she'd be caught. Boldly, she stepped forward, traversing the room, her heels sinking into the soft green carpet.

Janine had left the envelope square in the center of Damien's desk. Nothing else marred the surface and sunlight poured from the window, drawing immediate attention to the missive. It didn't have a mailing label—at a guess, it had been hand-delivered. A slashing masculine script had scrawled Damien's name across the front, and at the bottom 'private' had been printed, the word underlined twice. It had to be from Alex—there was no other reasonable explanation. But what had he written to Damien? She had to know.

Taking a deep breath, she reached out a trembling hand to pick it up.

'What do you think you're doing?' came Damien's voice from just behind her.

CHAPTER SEVEN

WITH a gasp, Sable whirled around, the petal-like scarves of her skirt flaring out around her. She lifted a trembling hand to her throat. 'You frightened me!'

'Did I?' Damien cocked an eyebrow, closing the distance between them. 'I wonder why? Doing something you shouldn't, sweetheart?'

She stared at him, her eyes huge and fearful. She didn't dare answer his question—not if she wanted to live. 'You could have given me some warning you were there,' she protested weakly, 'instead of sneaking up on me like that.'

'I could have. But since it's my office I didn't see the need.' He stopped inches from her, his height and breadth emphasized by his black silk suit, his wintry gaze more of a threat than she'd ever thought possible. If it was his intent to intimidate, he'd succeeded. Admirably. 'I repeat, what are you doing in here?'

'Just...just delivering some mail.' She gestured toward his desk. 'It got mixed in with mine.'

'The president of Caldwell's delivering mail.' His mouth tightened. 'What's wrong with that picture?'

He didn't believe her. She could see it in his face, in the clenched fists he held rigidly at his sides. She licked her lips and saw his eyes darken, saw the smoldering desire he couldn't quite suppress. And she knew what had to be done—no matter how much it went against the grain. Deliberately, she stepped away from the desk, hoping to draw his gaze from the incriminating envelope.

'You're right, of course,' she said with mocking lightness, throwing a provocative glance over her shoulder. 'I should have handed your mail over to Janine. That way you would have received it sometime Monday, instead of tonight.'

To her relief, he turned from the desk to watch the enticing sway of her hips and the seductive dance of the scarves as one moment they shifted to reveal an outrageous expanse of leg, and the next swirled closed.

He ran a hand through his damp hair, rumpling the tawny waves. 'What the hell are you wearing?' he demanded, his voice rough with emotion. He ripped his tie loose from his collar, flicking open the top two buttons of his dress shirt. The sophisticated businessman vanished, to be replaced by a man as tough and dangerous as he was irresistible. A man who watched her every move with savage intensity.

'Do you like it?' She paused in the doorway between their offices, leaning against the jam. The skirt parted again to flash a length of creamy white thigh.

He came after her then, moving with unmistakable purpose. She froze, her heart pounding wildly in her breast. Perhaps she'd played the role of the seductress a little too well. Clearly she'd started something he had every intention of finishing, even if she didn't. Color streaked across his cheekbones and a muscle jerked in his jaw. But it was the look in his eyes that held her immobile, her spine pressed rigidly to the wooden doorframe. He stared down at her with such passionate craving that his green eyes burned hot and iridescent. The next instant his hands closed around her shoulders and, with a muttered expletive, he dragged her into his arms.

'Damien, no! The reception!' she reminded him with a startled cry.

'Right now I don't give a damn about the reception. You asked for this. Hell, you practically begged for it. And I'm not about to refuse your invitation.'

His mouth closed over hers and white heat consumed her, desire kicking in harder and faster than ever before. With each renewed touch, each devastating kiss, her need for him grew, grew to monumental proportions. This had to stop, before she lost all control, before... Oh, God. Before she lost her heart to him all over again. Five years ago, he'd nearly destroyed her, his defection a shattering blow. She couldn't repeat the experience. She'd never survive it.

She wrenched her mouth from his, dragging air into her lungs in great, heaving gasps. 'We can't do this. Not here. Not now.' Not ever.

'Then when? You said you'd name the time and place. So name it.' His hand followed the line of her hip, slipping between the petals of her skirt until he found the smooth curve of her thigh. His fingers glided across her skin in slow, sensuous circles and her knees buckled, forcing her to cling to his shoulders. 'Tonight,' he urged. 'Come home with me tonight.'

She shook her head. 'I can't,' she murmured. His hand shifted slowly upward and her voice broke. 'Don't. Please, Damien.'

'Why the delay?' he demanded. 'You want me. Do you think I can't tell, that I don't see the desire in your eyes, feel you tremble every time I touch you?' He pressed closer, trapping her against the doorway. 'I know what you're feeling because I feel it too. I can't come near you without wanting to rip off your clothes.'

She turned her head to one side, her eyes squeezed shut. 'You don't just want me—you want revenge,' she protested, fighting to retain her sanity. 'Sometimes I think you want it more than anything else. You intend to use me and once you do, once you've had your satisfaction, you'll toss me out of your life again. Well, I can't let you treat me with such contempt. I don't deserve it.'

'Contempt?' His hand shifted from her shoulder, dropping to play across the upper swells of her breasts. 'Does this feel like contempt to you?'

No. It felt like heaven. She turned her head to look at him, her gaze direct and unflinching. 'Where will it lead, Damien? Once you have what you want, what then?'

She sensed his withdrawal and braced herself against the anguish sure to follow. His hand slid from her breast and she had her answer, without his ever having to say a word. He didn't want her—not on a permanent basis. Once he'd had his fill, he'd walk away. And no matter how much she tried to tell herself she didn't care, that he'd never kept the truth of his intentions from her, his silent acknowledgement was a torment beyond calculation. Oh, Damien, whatever happened to us? Who'd have believed it could ever come to this?

His gaze fastened on the ruby choker circling her neck and he reached out, running his thumb over the glittering stones. 'Caldwell let you keep this and the earrings?' he asked, his change of subject a welcome relief. 'I'm surprised.'

She shrugged, hoping the gesture looked casual, indifferent, that she successfully hid the desolation he'd wrought. 'Leonard didn't know I owned them,' she admitted.

He gave a short, harsh laugh. 'Let me guess. If he had known, he'd have suspected I'd given them to you. And once he'd realized they came from me he'd have sold them to help bail him out of his financial mess.'

'He'd probably have considered it poetic justice,' she admitted.

'And damn your feelings on the matter?'

'Possibly,' she conceded. Unquestionably. 'But they belonged to me, not him.' And she couldn't bear to part with them.

Damien's mouth curved. 'Yeah, well, Lenny liked taking things that didn't belong to him. I'm glad you kept them. They suit you. So does the dress for that matter.'

'Thank you,' she said lightly. 'And now, if you'll give me a minute to freshen up, I think it's time we went down to the party. We're already five minutes late.' And heaven only knew what their employees and guests would make of that. Whatever they thought, it wouldn't be far from the truth.

His hand gripped her elbow, preventing her from moving. 'You still haven't told me where or when.'

'No, I haven't, have I?' He wasn't slow on the uptake; nor did he bother to hide his displeasure. She pulled from his grasp and stepped away from the door, turning her back on him. She could feel his eyes boring into her spine.

'Sable.' He waited until he'd captured her attention, his expression stern and ruthless. 'Just so you know... I keep all the bid information locked in a safe.'

Fierce color heated her cheeks and in that moment she almost hated him. The irony of it made her want to weep. She hadn't been after the bids, but the whole purpose of her venture into his office had been equally damning—

to steal Alex's envelope. She couldn't very well protest her innocence when she had so much to feel guilty about.

'I'll keep that in mind for future reference,' she said coolly, and disappeared into her bathroom, using the precious moments afforded her to recover her poise.

Five minutes later they entered the party and it proved every bit as bad as Sable had feared. All eyes turned in their direction, a momentary hush descending on the gathering. She faltered just enough for Damien to notice.

'What's wrong?'

'Sorry,' she murmured, making a swift recovery. 'All the attention threw me for just a moment.'

His brows drew together. 'You're chairman of the board, president of Caldwell's. You must be used to this sort of attention by now.'

'Perhaps I should have said infamy rather than attention,' she said in a dry undertone.

'If you're infamous, you have only yourself to blame,' he retorted with a noteworthy lack of sympathy.

'So you keep telling me.'

Her spine ramrod-stiff and her head held high, she swept down the stairs to the ballroom as she'd done innumerable times before. She wouldn't allow them to defeat her, to intimidate her.

To her utter astonishment, Damien gained her side before she'd gone more than two steps. His arm slipped around her, his hand planted square in the middle of her back. The gesture was duly noted. He might as well have put a sign around her neck, proclaiming that she had his protection. It meant more to her than she could possibly express, but it provided a false sense of security. She couldn't trust that he'd protect her. After all... he hadn't before.

The next two hours proved the most difficult of Sable's life. She greeted Caldwell's clients, introduced Damien, and then forced herself to stand passively at his side while he seized the conversational ball. It didn't take anyone long to figure out that the winds of change were sweeping through the company, and that Damien was the force behind those winds.

She met the speculative looks with a false calm, deflected the barbed comments with pleasant smiles, and cloaked herself behind a facade that even the most objectional remark couldn't penetrate. But all the while she retreated emotionally, withdrawing further and further, determined to keep a small, innermost part of herself safe from harm.

The worse moment of the evening occurred when they crossed paths with Patricia, who'd come as the guest of one of their clients. Sable stared at her former sister-in-law in disbelief, stunned by the sheer audacity of the woman. She'd sold Caldwell's down the river, yet joined in the discussion as though nothing had changed.

'So,' Patricia said during a lull in the conversation, 'how did you enjoy your moment of power heading Caldwell's? Or didn't it last long enough to enjoy?'

Sable didn't bother to dignify the question with a response. 'I'm surprised you have the nerve to show up here,' she said instead.

'Why? I've done nothing to be ashamed of.' Patricia lifted an eyebrow. 'Have you?'

A worried-looking Janine joined the small group at that point, forestalling Sable's reply. 'Excuse me, Mrs Caldwell. With all the confusion earlier I forgot to deliver a message—from Kyle.'

Sable stiffened, not daring to look in Damien's direction. But she didn't doubt for a minute that she had his undivided attention. 'Was it urgent?'

'I don't believe so. He did ask that you phone home.'

'Thank you, Janine. I'll return his call in a few minutes.'

'And how is Kyle?' Patricia questioned, slanting a knowing smile in Damien's direction.

Sable struggled to remain calm. If she revealed even the slightest hint of panic, her former sister-in-law would take malicious delight in disclosing precisely who Kyle was. 'He's fine,' she replied steadily.

Patricia turned to Damien. 'Have you met him?' she asked with mock-innocence.

'Not yet.'

The brevity of his response spoke volumes and amusement gleamed in Patricia's eyes. 'Yes, Sable does like to keep him all to herself. You'll have to get her to introduce you some time. I think you'd find it well worth your while.'

It was the last straw, and Sable's composure shattered. 'That's enough, Patricia!' she snapped, instantly regretting her loss of control. All eyes focused on her and she fought to regain her equilibrium, offering a remote smile. 'If you'll excuse me, I have a phone call to make.' And with that she turned on her heel and hastened from the room. She had to get away, had to escape before she betrayed herself any further.

Returning to her office, she placed a quick call home. Millie picked up the phone, her calm greeting going a long way toward soothing Sable's agitation. 'He called you?' the nanny questioned in astonishment. 'The little rascal! I had no idea he knew your work number.'

'But everything's all right?'

'Just fine. I put him to bed over an hour ago and haven't heard a peep out of him.'

'Thank you, Millie. I should be home soon.'

Ringing off, Sable rubbed her temples, the beginnings of a headache setting in. She hesitated, glancing in the direction of Damien's office. If she intended to get a look at Alex's communiqué, it was now or never. Taking a deep breath, she crossed the room and pushed open the door. This time she didn't hesitate, but hurried directly to Damien's desk and picked up the envelope.

She wanted to rip it open. She wanted to destroy it before Damien had a chance to read the contents. But at the last moment she knew she couldn't do it. No matter what anyone believed, she hadn't leaked the bids. To do so would have gone against ever tenet she'd ever held dear. And so did this. That decided, she opened her hand, allowing the envelope to flutter back to the desk.

'So it wasn't the bids you were after earlier.'

Swearing beneath her breath, she slowly swiveled to face Damien. He stood, leaning against the doorjamb, his arms folded across his chest. She looked at him and shuddered. His face was dark and forbidding, his eyes the only thing revealing any expression—and those glittered with a white-hot rage. She'd made a serious error in judgement and soon she'd pay for that error.

'No, I wasn't interested in the bids,' she replied with amazing composure.

'What's in the envelope?'

'I don't know. I couldn't bring myself to open it.'

'Give it to me.' He held out his hand and, with no other alternative, she picked up the envelope and relinquished it to him. 'Shall we go?'

She didn't dare argue, not when his fury simmered just below the surface, ready to explode with volcanic force at the first sign of opposition. 'Go where?'

'Back to the party,' he informed her tautly. 'It's on the verge of breaking up. We'll stand there—together— until the last person has left and then we'll leave.'

'We'. The two of them. Her hands curled into fists. 'And then?'

'I'll take you home.' His expression flayed her. '*Then* we'll open the envelope and see what you're so desperate to keep from me.'

It was as though all her emotions had iced over. She couldn't think, couldn't feel, couldn't comprehend the fact that total disaster awaited around the next bend. She might as well have been an automaton. Without protest, she returned with him to the party and stood at his side until the room had cleared. She smiled. She shook hands. She even managed to string words together into complete sentences. She must have made sense, since no one seemed to notice anything amiss.

And all the while Damien stood at her side. He kept the incriminating envelope rolled in his fist, slapping it relentlessly against his thigh. If his intention was to drive her to the brink of insanity, he was unquestionably succeeding. By the time he decided to leave, her nerves were shredded. It wasn't until he'd assisted her into his black Jaguar that she came to life.

'I don't want you coming home with me,' she began.

'Tough.'

'I'm serious, Damien. You can't come in.'

He stopped at a stop sign and glanced at her, the lights from the dash playing across his taut, unforgiving features. 'I'm coming in.'

She shook her head. 'Not a chance.'

He accelerated through the intersection, and started up a hill, shifting gears with the ease of long practice. 'You either agree or I continue on to Sausalito. And if we do that, count on it that you won't need to worry any more about where or when we make love. The decision will be out of your hands.'

She inhaled sharply. 'You can't do that!' she protested. 'You promised.'

'I can and I will. And you won't fight me about it, either. At least, not for long. Not if your response earlier is any indication.'

'That's a foul thing to say!'

'It's honest and it's accurate.' He shot her an impatient look. 'Now which will it be? My place or yours? Decide before this light changes or I'll make the decision for you.'

It didn't take any thought. There was only one choice. She sent up a small prayer that Millie had made Kyle pick up before going to bed. Otherwise they'd be discussing far more than just the contents of that envelope. 'Take me home,' she finally said.

His laugh held a sardonic edge. 'Now why doesn't that surprise me?'

She didn't speak for the rest of the drive. He parked outside her house, curbing the wheels and setting the emergency brake. She didn't wait for him to open her door. All things considered, the small courtesy would be painfully out of place. Damien followed her up the steps to the porch, waiting impatiently at her side while she unlocked the front door. Walking in behind her, his footsteps echoed on the inlaid oak flooring. Sable glanced up the steps leading to the bedrooms. Millie had apparently retired for the evening; all was quiet.

'Lenny had good taste,' Damien commented. 'A bit of a comedown from Gopher's Hole, of course——'

'Fox's Lair!'

He shrugged. 'Whatever. When was this place built? 1906? 1907?'

'1907. Right after the earthquake. And Leonard didn't choose the house, I did—a month after he died.' She tossed her purse on to the hall table. 'Now, are we through with the pleasant chit-chat or shall we debate whether the leaded windows are originals? Or, if you'd prefer, we could marvel over the fact that the framework and upstairs flooring are made from redwood.' She lifted her chin. 'Well?'

His gaze settled on her face and she wondered if he could see the tension in her expression, sense her exhaustion. 'What I'd like is a cup of coffee,' he finally said.

'Excuse me?'

'Coffee. That amazing bean they grow in South America and ship here. You know. Grind it. Brew it. Drink it.'

'I know what coffee is! I just don't understand. I thought you'd want...' She gestured toward the envelope fisted in his hand.

His mouth tightened. 'Oh, we'll get to that soon enough. But first...coffee.'

There was no point in arguing. But she wondered if this wasn't a delaying tactic. Did he hope the mysterious Kyle would choose to join them? Heavens, he'd better not. She shot a surreptitious glance toward the living room. It appeared tidy enough, none of her son's toys readily apparent. She'd just have to risk it.

'Have a seat, I'll be right back,' she said, and headed for the kitchen. Moving as swiftly as possible, she scooped a blend of her favorite coffee into the coffee maker. Next, she removed two mugs form the cupboard and set them on the counter.

'Anything I can do to help?' Damien asked, appearing in the doorway.

She froze, shooting a sudden, panicked glance toward the refrigerator—a refrigerator plastered with Kyle's artwork. 'Not a thing. I'll join you in a minute.' Take the hint! she willed silently. And get out of my kitchen. The coffee maker burbled and a final drop of coffee plopped into the glass carafe. Snatching up the mugs, she filled them to the brim. 'Let's go,' she urged.

His brows drew together. 'I thought you preferred half coffee, half cream.'

'I decided to take a leaf from your book and try it straight up and uncorrupted,' she said as calmly as she could manage.

A smile edged across his mouth. 'Black?'

'Black,' she confirmed, moving toward the living room. 'Shall we?' He didn't protest, nor did he look in the direction of the refrigerator. She could have cried with relief.

'I wouldn't think you'd be so eager to open this envelope. Nor hear what I have to say about your efforts to steal it.'

A thousand possible comebacks flashed through her mind, not one of any use. After all, she *had* planned to steal the envelope. She couldn't very well deny it. Even explaining that she'd changed her mind would be pointless, merely underlining her initial guilt. 'I'd rather get this over with,' she said with a frustrated sigh. 'Besides, I'd like to find out what's in there, too.'

'You don't know?'

'I have my suspicions.' She sat down on the couch, cradling the mug between her hands. And that was when she saw it.

On the carpet at her feet lay one of Kyle's shoes.

She choked.

'Something wrong?' Damien questioned.

'Coasters! Could you...could you hand me a coaster, please? They're on the end table beside you.' The minute he turned, she scooped up the telltale evidence and thrust it between the cushion and the arm of the couch. Frantically, she looked around for the shoe's mate. Knowing Kyle, it could be anywhere.

He handed her the wooden coaster. 'Lose something?'

'Yes. *No!*' To her abject horror, tears of desperation flooded her eyes. Terrified that he'd notice her loss of control, she lowered her head and took a hasty sip of coffee. Without the cream to cool it, it scalded her tongue, and she gasped at the pain, the breath sobbing beneath her lips. She blinked rapidly. At least now she'd have an excuse for her tears.

Damien reached out and took the mug from her trembling hands, setting it on the coaster. 'Calm down,' he told her quietly. 'Getting upset isn't going to change anything. Now let's get this over with.' And in one swift move he ripped open the envelope.

She flinched at the sound. 'Well? What does Alex say?'

'He confirms that someone at Caldwell's is leaking information, and as proof has sent a copy of the prospectus we prepared for Luther.' He studied the papers. 'This is our bid, there's no question about that. It came from our office.'

'Why would he send it to you?' she asked with a frown. 'It doesn't make sense. Couldn't you pursue legal action against him?'

Damien shook his head. 'He knows I won't, that all I want is the person at Caldwell's who's stealing the information. As to why he'd help me...' His mouth twisted. 'I imagine that as long as you and Patricia headed the company he didn't have many qualms about helping himself to this information.'

'But once you came on board all that changed?' The sheer audacity of it took her breath away. 'It's all right to steal from women, but not from men?' she questioned incredulously.

'If you and Patricia had acted the first time this had happened, he wouldn't have thought that,' Damien retorted sharply. 'Instead you let it be known that Caldwell's was an easy mark. But Alex knows me. He knows I won't stand still for theft, that I'll uncover the truth, no matter who I have to take down to do it. He's just throwing me a bone and moving out of the way, hoping I won't come after him.'

It made sense. Unfortunately. 'Did he... did he add anything else?'

'Yes.' Damien's gaze locked with hers. 'He suggests I watch my back.'

She licked her lips. 'But what about the person who leaked the information? Does... does he say who it is?'

'Not in so many words. But he doesn't have to.' He tossed Alex's papers on to the coffee table in front of them. 'Tell me, Sable, why did you think he'd pin it on you? What proof does he have?'

'I... I don't understand.'

'Yes, you do. You tried to get hold of Alex's letter, not once but twice. You're terrified. I see it in your eyes. I can hear it in your voice. He must have some sort of evidence of your involvement or you wouldn't have been so desperate to get your hands on this envelope.'

'He doesn't have any proof!' she cried. 'He can't.'

'Then why are you so frightened? What's going on?'

She bowed her head. 'I don't know,' she confessed. 'I wish I did.'

He thrust a hand through his hair and got to his feet, crossing to stand by the fireplace grate. Stripping off his suit coat, he slung it over the arm of a nearby chair. Next, he loosened the dark red tie at his throat. He couldn't have stated his intentions more clearly. He planned to stay as long as it took in order to get to the bottom of this situation.

He faced her, the snowy-white dress shirt clinging to the full, muscular expanse of his shoulders. His jaw was clenched, and he thrust his hands into his trouser pockets, the black silk pulled taut across his thighs. His movements were filled with a volatile impatience, as though he barely held himself in check.

'Let's begin again,' he bit out. 'You don't seem to realize how close you are to disaster. I suggest you be frank with me, while you still have the chance.'

Her gaze jerked upward. 'Is that a threat?'

'It's a promise. Now what does Alex Johnson have on you? How are you involved?'

Perhaps he was right. Perhaps the time had come to level with him. Damien wasn't joking. Without question he planned to seek legal action against the person responsible. She had to find a way to convince him of her innocence or she'd take the fall.

'All right, Damien. I'll tell you what I know.' She struggled to gather her thoughts, trying to determine the best place to start. At the beginning seemed sensible. 'After Leonard's death last year, Patricia took over as chairwoman, and we started losing the occasional contract. None of us thought much of it. I mean, you can't win them all. Ryan Matheson expressed concern, but Patricia refused to listen. And since she was in control...' Sable sighed. 'The rest of us fell into line.'

'So the problem was ignored?'

'Yes,' she confessed. Looking back, the decision seemed foolish in the extreme. But at the time... 'After this last board meeting, Ryan approached me, warning that there were rumors of a leak.'

'And warning that that fact would figure in his report?'

'Figure predominately.' She met his eyes without flinching. 'I swear to you, Damien, it never occurred to me there might be a leak. It seems so obvious now. But then...' She shrugged helplessly. 'Right after my meeting with Ryan, I decided to try and find out who was to blame. I hoped to uncover the guilty party before Ryan completed his report to you.'

She couldn't tell if her confession angered him. He stood quietly, listening intently, his face expressionless. 'So, what did you do?'

'I asked Ryan to prepare a list of all possible suspects—anyone who'd had access to the information. And then I called Alex Johnson and asked him to name his source.'

Damien released a bark of laughter. 'Did you really think he'd tell you?' he asked in disbelief.

Warm color swept into her cheeks. 'No. But I hoped he'd say something that might clue me in.'

'And did he?'

'Alex was very generous,' she admitted huskily. 'He told me precisely who had leaked the information.'

Damien straightened, his gaze sharpening. 'And?'

She plucked at the filmy scarves of her skirt. It was all so hopeless. 'He said I had leaked the information.'

'He *what*?'

'He said I had leaked the information,' she repeated stoically.

His eyes flamed and his hands clenched into fists. 'And did you?'

'*No!*' She bit down on her lip, quickly lowering her voice. If Kyle heard her, he'd be downstairs like a shot. 'Of course I didn't. But what's so frightening is...I believed him, Damien. Alex isn't lying when he says it's me. I mean, I'm not guilty, but he's convinced I'm responsible.'

Damien turned slightly, staring into the empty fireplace grate, his brows drawn together in a fierce frown. 'Have you any idea why he might think that?' he questioned.

'I have an idea.' She hesitated, not certain that she wanted to discuss it. 'But I have no proof. It's just a suspicion.'

'Tell me,' he ordered.

'Patricia's last name is also Caldwell. Perhaps he confused us.' Spoken aloud it seemed totally inane.

Apparently Damien thought so too. He shook his head. 'Alex isn't stupid. Sorry, Sable. It's too convenient. Wasn't she the one you pointed the finger at last time?'

Her mouth tightened. 'You asked and I've told you. She kept the board from investigating the problem sooner. She had access to the Luther bid. Maybe Alex just heard the name Caldwell and assumed it was me.'

'Why would he think that?'

'For the same reason everyone else assumes it,' she retorted. 'My reputation precedes me.'

'But why would Patricia leak the information? What's her motivation?'

Sable shrugged. 'To get even? She sold her shares of Caldwell's to you because the board removed her as chairwoman. Once she'd sold out, I suspect she'd think it served us right if the company lost business. And there's one other reason. She's always held us responsible for destroying both her brother and her family's business. Not that I entirely blame her for feeling that way.'

He turned then, his face set in hard, implacable lines. 'There's one way of knowing for sure whether or not she's guilty.'

'Which is?'

'She no longer has access to company files. Therefore, if she's responsible, the Luther development should be the last bid that's leaked.'

She couldn't fault his logic. But for some reason her fear didn't ease. 'Assuming she's the one who did it,' Sable murmured.

Damien's smile made her very, very nervous. 'You've sworn you're innocent. So, who else could it possibly be?'

A tiny sound distracted her, a sound only a mother would notice—the stealthy turning of a doorknob. She hastened to her feet, the petals of her skirt fluttering about her knees in an agitated swirl. 'Is there anything else?' she asked, struggling to conceal her panic. 'I'd like to call it a night, if you don't mind.'

He tilted his head to one side, his eyes narrowing. 'And if I do mind?'

She gripped her hands together, desperate to get rid of him. 'I've answered your questions to the best of my knowledge. I think we should sleep on it.'

'What a good idea.' He started across the room and she saw desire flare to life in his eyes. She knew that look—and knew where it would lead.

'No,' she whispered in dismay. 'Oh, no! I meant sleep on it and...and discuss it further in the morning.' She darted across the room and snatched up his coat. Keeping him at arm's length, she hurried toward the foyer.

Damien followed. Just as they reached the entranceway, he dropped a hand on her shoulder and spun her around. 'What's going on, Sable? What's your hurry?'

A floorboard creaked, the sort of sound a house made when it settled for the night...or the sound a small boy made when he was sneaking down the hallway. If Damien heard, he gave no indication. 'I'm exhausted.' She faked a yawn. 'See? It's time for you to go.' She grabbed at the doorknob, jerking desperately at it until it finally opened.

He leaned a shoulder against the oak door and it crashed closed again. 'I'm not leaving. Not without this.' Before she could react, he pulled her into his arms and kissed her.

Even knowing that Kyle was slipping ever closer to the stairway behind them, even knowing that at any moment disaster would strike and her worse nightmare would be realized, she couldn't help but respond. Her hands crept up his chest, circling his shoulders, and she clung to him, opened to him, returned his kiss with a passion she couldn't deny. When he finally released her, every thought in her head had vanished. She could only stare up at him, her eyes huge and wonder-struck.

Thunk.

Her brow wrinkled, reality slowly returning. She knew that sound. Kyle made it when he slid, step by step, down the stairs. *Kyle!* She didn't waste another moment. With a gasp, she ripped free of Damien's arms and attacked the door again. Finally, *finally* it opened. 'We'll talk in the morning,' she cried. She thrust Damien's coat into his hands and shoved at his chest with all her might.

Thunk.

To her astonished relief, he took a step backward over the threshold. She didn't think twice. She slammed the door in his face. Turning, she saw how close she'd been to total calamity. Kyle slid into view, his face wreathed in an ear-to-ear grin.

'Mommy!' he shouted.

She hastened to the steps, scooping him up into her arms. 'I missed you,' she whispered, hugging him close. Thank heavens. Oh, thank heavens she'd been in time.

Or so she thought.

The door squeaked open behind her.

'I assume this is Kyle,' came Damien's dry voice.

CHAPTER EIGHT

DAMIEN leaned against the front door, his cool, watchful gaze sweeping over Sable, before settling on Kyle. 'It would seem we have more to discuss than just that envelope. No wonder you were in such a hurry to get rid of me.'

Sable's grip tightened around her son. 'How did you know?' she whispered. 'How did you know to come back in?'

Damien reached into the pocket of his suit coat and he tugged out Kyle's shoe. The sneaker rested on his palm, looking absurdly small compared with his hand. 'I believe this matches the one you shoved under the couch cushion.'

So he'd seen, had known all along. She closed her eyes, her distress increasing by the minute. 'I have to put Kyle to bed.'

He couldn't seem to stop staring at the boy. Not that Kyle minded. He returned the scrutiny with equal intensity. 'He's your son.' It wasn't a question.

There was no point in denying it. The truth was self-evident. 'Yes, he's my son,' she confirmed.

Her agitation grew to an unbearable level and she stood, lifting Kyle into her arms. He'd gotten too old and heavy to carry like this, but she dreaded what Damien might do...might say. She was terrified that he would ask that all-important question. And she didn't want her son—their son—present when it happened.

Kyle wrapped his arms around her neck and his legs about her waist, content to watch and listen. He showed no fear, no shyness. She knew he was busy weighing up the situation—and the man. As soon as he'd formed an opinion, he wouldn't hesitate to express it, for good or bad. Just like his father.

'He looks like you.' Damien broke the prolonged silence. He glanced at the sneaker, seeming surprised to discover he still held it. Crossing to the hall table, he set it gently beside her purse. 'As soon as I found the shoe, I realized Kyle had to be a child. But I couldn't be certain he was yours. You'd told me he was a relative. That covers a lot of ground.'

'So, now you know.'

'Yes. Now I know.' He stood—tense, wary. He'd wandered into uncharted territory and wouldn't begin his attack until he'd completed his analysis of the situation.

She didn't dare afford him the time for that analysis. 'I need to go upstairs now,' she informed him, not caring if she sounded abrupt. 'I'll see you on Monday.'

'Wait.' He held out a hand, as though to detain her physically. Then he pulled back, thrusting his fist into his trouser pocket, his eyes darkening with some turbulent emotion. 'Wait for just a minute, if you would.'

For a crazy instant she thought his expression showed a momentary regret, a flash of longing. But she knew she must be mistaken. Damien experiencing regret? Damien needing something or someone? Not a chance. He didn't need anyone. Not her. And not her son. 'What do you want?' she asked. 'It's late and I'm tired. I'd rather we continue this another time.'

'I'm sure you would. But I wouldn't. Tell me, Sable—why the big secret?' he demanded. 'Why go to such extreme lengths to keep me from finding out?'

His momentary hesitation had vanished, replaced by unmistakable strength and authority. This was the Damien she knew so well. He watched her keenly and she couldn't get an image out of her mind—an image of a jungle cat catching wind of his prey. She had to flee. Now. Before it was too late, before he'd made up his mind whether or not to give chase. 'This isn't the appropriate time for questions, Damien. I...I have to put Kyle to bed.'

'May I join you?'

That he'd ask permission instead of demand the right revealed just how moved he was by Kyle. But she couldn't allow compassion to influence her judgement. 'I don't think that would be a good idea,' she began.

Kyle turned his head, his mouth close to her ear, and whispered, 'He can come. Day-man can come.'

She bit down on her lip, his mispronunciation of Damien's name as deeply affecting as his request. She wished she could refuse, wished she could race up the stairs and escape the coming discussion. 'It would seem that I've been overruled,' she said, darting a swift, reluctant look at Damien. 'Kyle would like it if you'd tuck him in for the night.'

Man and boy exchanged a long look, a look that excluded her, a look of complete understanding. Damien inclined his head. 'Thank you. I'd like that.' He glanced at her. 'He's too heavy for you to carry. Let me take him.'

Without a moment's hesitation, Kyle held out his arms, and, with no other choice, she relinquished her son. *Their* son, she reminded herself yet again. It was time she faced facts. Damien and Kyle belonged together. She'd always known it, always resisted that knowledge because she was afraid. Afraid that Damien would want her son—but wouldn't want her. They ascended the stairs together, almost like a family. It was a treacherous thought, an unrealistic thought.

'Which way?' he asked at the top of the steps.

'The first room.' She gestured to the right and moved ahead of them, pushing open the door to Kyle's bedroom. 'In here.'

Damien looked around. 'Nice,' he approved. 'Why the bunk beds?'

'For friends,' Kyle answered the question for her. 'And 'cuz I like it. The top is my fort.' He pointed at the ceiling. 'See the stars?'

Damien tilted back his head. A whole galaxy of glittering stars and planets, applied with glow-in-the-dark paint, spread across the ceiling. 'Clever.'

'And the bottom is my cave.' He wiggled free of Damien's arms and clambered on to the lower bunk. 'See? I put blankets all around so it's dark. And Mommy lets me draw on the wall like a real caveman.'

'She does, does she?' He shot her an amused look.

'It's only the one wall,' she murmured. 'And it saved the rest of the walls in the house from any further artistic endeavors.' She turned her attention to her son. 'It's time for bed, sweetheart. Where are you sleeping tonight? You need to choose.'

Kyle settled cross-legged on the mattress, his brows drawn together in thought. Sable caught her breath. He looked so much like his father, it was frightening. She glanced nervously at Damien. Did he suspect the truth? Did he see himself mirrored in those miniature features? If so, he gave no sign.

'Here. In the cave,' Kyle decided, and burrowed beneath the sheet. 'But I wants Day-man to tuck me in.'

Damien didn't wait for a second invitation. He dropped to one knee beside the bed. With a giggle, Kyle kicked off the sheet and for the next few minutes a wrestling match ensued. Damien made a big production of pulling up the covers and tucking them beneath the squirming little boy. The instant he finished, Kyle churned his arms and legs until the bedcovers were strewn half on and half off the bed. With a growl of mock-fury, Damien would then start the process all over again. Inevitably, Kyle tired and finally gave in to Damien's persistence, allowing the sheet and blanket to stay put.

Damien ruffled the boy's dark curls, the gesture tender beyond belief. 'How old are you, Kyle?' he questioned unexpectedly.

Alarm streaked through Sable and she stepped forward. 'Please, don't——' she began.

'Six,' came the sleepy retort, though with his lisp it sounded more like 'thix'.

'Six?' Damien repeated, lifting an eyebrow.

Velvety eyes opened, the ebony depths twinkling with laughter. His smile widened into a grin. 'I'm gonna be six. I'm gonna be six t'morrow. Right, Mommy?'

Sable smiled, relaxing ever so slightly. 'If you want to be.'

His freckled nose wrinkled. 'Maybe I'll be ten. Or a lion.' He bared his tiny teeth and curled his fingers into claws. 'I can growl real good.'

'I'm sure you can,' Damien agreed with a husky laugh. 'Goodnight.'

'You gonna come tomorrow?' Kyle asked. 'You can if you wants to.'

'Thanks. I'd like that. But if I don't see you tomorrow, I'll see you again soon. OK?' It was the perfect response. Kyle readily agreed, and, with a huge yawn, curled into a tight ball, his lids drifting closed.

Without a sound, Damien and Sable crept from the room. Neither spoke as they returned to the living room. She glanced at him, considering what she'd say, how she'd explain the truth so that he'd understand, so that he wouldn't hate her. He wasn't going to take this well, and she couldn't blame him. They should have had this little talk years ago.

He took up his stance by the fireplace again, his profile turned to her, one hand planted on the mantel as he stared down at the slate hearth. She knew he was gathering his thoughts for the coming discussion, and she stared at him, drinking in the strong sweep of his brow, the taut, angled curve of his cheekbones, the firm, determined chin and passionate mouth.

She caught her breath in dismay. She loved him, she realized then, the knowledge as stunning as it was undeniable. She'd never stopped loving him. Even when he'd hurt her, when he'd withdrawn his support, her feelings had never truly died, only been buried. All these years. All these long, lonely years she'd kept her emotions on ice, refusing to allow anyone close—except Kyle.

And now she knew why. Because throughout that time she'd held on to the secret hope that she and Damien would have another opportunity, that there would come a time when they'd find each other again. She closed her eyes. And now that they finally had, any chance of them working out their problems was doomed to fail. He wouldn't forgive her for keeping Kyle a secret, any more than he'd forgiven her for betraying him. The knowledge came as a devastating blow.

She glanced at him, exhaustion slipping over her, and she struggled to conceal her regret... and her yearning. 'Is it really necessary to go into this tonight?' she questioned. She could predict his answer, but hoped that he might relent and let her off the hook.

He turned his head, an unexpected smile touching his mouth. 'You've been ducking this conversation since I bought into Caldwell's,' he told her drily. His amusement died, his eyes darkening with emotion. 'He's a beautiful child, Sable. But he's not six. How old is he?'

She sank to the couch, burying her hands in the filmy layers of her skirt. So now it began. 'Four,' she told him, without delay or evasion.

'Four...?' He stilled, a sudden, savage light growing in his eyes. 'Four... or four and a few months?'

She knew the point of the question. If Kyle was just four, he would be Leonard's son. If he was more than that... 'Four and a few months,' she whispered.

He didn't react, didn't show any emotion. But a vein throbbed in his temple and the muscles in his jaw clenched, warning that he wasn't as calm as he appeared. 'Kyle's the reason you married, isn't he?'

She nodded, her heart pounding. 'Yes,' she admitted, waiting for the other shoe to drop, for him to draw the ultimate conclusion.

'You were already pregnant when you married Caldwell, weren't you?'

'Yes,' she repeated.

Fury erupted, sweeping across his face like a dark tide. She could see him fight it, struggling to keep his temper in check. He didn't succeed. 'Six weeks after leaving me you were pregnant and married to that son of a bitch? Six *weeks*!'

She stared in bewilderment, confused by what he'd said. He couldn't believe.... He didn't think that Kyle was *Leonard's*, did he? 'Damien, wait a minute. You have it all wrong. I can explain——'

'Explain! Explain what?' He straightened, stepping away from the mantel, and she stiffened, the unadulterated rage in his expression causing her to shrink back against the cushions. 'I won't bother asking if there's any chance Kyle's mine.'

'*What*?'

'Oh, don't look so insulted.' He thrust a hand through his hair, the movement filled with barely suppressed violence. 'Hell, it must have been a close thing, a matter of weeks between the time you left my bed and crawled into Caldwell's. There had to have been a momentary doubt over who fathered your child. I'm surprised it didn't occur to Lenny. Considering his lack of principles, I'm amazed he was willing to marry you at all. He had to have been damned certain the kid was his. How did you convince him? Or didn't he know about us?'

He couldn't have shocked her more if he'd slapped her. 'You bastard!' she whispered.

'That's why you were so anxious to keep Kyle a secret, wasn't it? Once I knew about him, you had to realize I'd suspect the rest—that you were in cahoots with Caldwell from the start, sleeping with him, supplying him with bid information.'

'No!'

He came closer. 'No, you weren't conspiring with Lenny, supplying him with bid information?' he ripped into her. 'Or no, you weren't sleeping with him?'

She leapt to her feet, determined not to cower on the couch, refusing to show any weakness or vulnerability that he could twist to his advantage. 'I never told Leonard anything about your contracts or your clients. I let certain facts slip to Patricia, I've never denied that. But I never, ever discussed Hawke Enterprises with Leonard. Nor was I sleeping with him.'

'Well, if you weren't sleeping with Lenny before the leaks, you sure as hell had to be sleeping with him right afterward. Your son's proof enough of that.' His sarcasm cut her to the quick.

'You've got it all wrong!' she protested.

'Then why did you keep Kyle's existence a secret these past two weeks?'

'Why in the world would I want to tell you about him?' she shot back. 'Why would I tell you when it would give you one more weapon to use against me in this little vendetta of yours?'

'You think I'd use a child? That I'd ever do anything to harm your son?' His affront would have been laughable if matters weren't so heartbreaking.

'That's precisely what I think. You'd do anything and everything in your power to hurt me; that's the whole reason you bought into Caldwell's. Why would I think you'd make an exception for Kyle?' she demanded. 'What have you done that could possibly lead me to believe that?'

'Don't you dare dump this on me,' he bit out. 'What the hell was I supposed to believe? You've lied to me from the beginning. About the bids. About Caldwell. About your own son.'

'I haven't! I've been trying to tell you——'

He snatched her into his arms then, his body taut and hard, his anger a tangible force. 'Have you any idea what it does to me, knowing you allowed that piece of slime to touch you? Knowing he fathered a child with you?'

Tears clogged her throat, making it a struggle to speak, but she had to explain, had to make him understand what she'd gone through, how she'd felt. 'He was good to me at a time I had nowhere to turn. You had deserted me. I was unemployed and alone. If it hadn't been for Leonard...' Her voice broke, distress heavy in her voice.

'All I know is that you betrayed me. Of all the things you could have done, you chose the one I could never forgive.' His hands slid across her bared shoulders, slipping upward to cup her face. 'Kyle could have been our son. Has that ever occurred to you?'

The truth trembled on her lips, and almost—almost— she confessed everything. 'Damien, I have to tell you——'

He shook his head. 'You don't have to say another word.' His expression might have been carved from granite. 'The facts speak for themselves. If you hadn't been so greedy, so treacherous, Kyle could have been mine.'

Tears threatened to overwhelm her. Was that what he really thought of her? 'And what if he had been?' she asked. 'What then?'

His passion, his fury, broke free. 'Then I could have watched you ripen with my child. I could have been there when you gave birth to him, seen him suckle at your breast, been a father to him. Instead you took all that from me and gave the privilege to another man.'

She inhaled sharply. 'You hate the idea that he could be Leonard's, don't you? You hate Kyle because of who his father might be.'

'I want to hate you both,' came the furious response. He closed his eyes, fighting some inner demon, the anger slowly draining away. 'But I can't. Not after seeing Kyle, touching him, hearing his laugh. Dear God, Sable.' The pain in his voice was nearly her undoing. 'He could have been ours.'

'No, he couldn't have been,' she told him raggedly. 'Because you don't want a real son, let alone a real wife. You want someone without failings, someone perfect, without flaw or human foibles. Well, we can never be like that. For Kyle to be your son would mean letting down your guard and trusting, risking your heart. And for me to be your wife would mean believing in me despite all evidence to the contrary. And you've never been willing or able to do that, have you?'

He didn't deny it. 'And Caldwell was?' he asked instead.

'Yes,' she retorted without hesitation. 'For all his faults, Leonard loved Kyle unconditionally, without a moment's reservation. And he defended me, believed in me when no one else would. And I'll always be grateful to him for that.'

'Grateful?' He instantly honed in on the word. 'Is that what you felt for Leonard? What about love? Or wasn't that important to you?'

She didn't pretend to misunderstand. 'I love Kyle. That's more than enough.'

'Is it?' His voice dropped, grew husky and seductive, and his hands slipped deep into her hair. 'Are you sure?'

She licked her lips, her gaze slipping from his. 'Positive.'

'Let's see if I can't change your mind about that.'

His thumb drifted across her mouth, teasing her lips apart. And then he took them with his, delving within, tasting with a deftness and delicacy that stole her heart yet again. She couldn't help capitulating, offering up her mouth in sweet surrender. He held her with a tenderness that made resistance impossible, exploring with barely restrained passion, his gentle seduction doing far more to sweep aside any lingering doubts than a more determined assault.

'Tell me what you want,' he murmured, his mouth drifting to the sensitive juncture between her neck and shoulder. 'Tell me you want me—want me here and now. There's no point in waiting any longer. You know Caldwell never made you feel like this, that you never came close to sharing with him what we once had. Let me prove it to you.'

She stiffened, pulling back, sanity slowly returning. 'Is that the point of all this? To prove you're a better lover than Leonard?'

He shook his head. 'I don't need to prove it. You already know what we shared was unique. It's not something we'll find again. You just don't want to admit it because of Kyle, because it might hurt him to know that Caldwell didn't measure up. So you've made your husband into a saint, someone Kyle can be proud of. But he wasn't. There's a lot you don't know about the man.'

Anger stirred. 'And you intend to tell me, is that it?'

'No. It won't change anything for you to know.' He released her. 'You're not in the mood to continue this, so I'll leave. But I want you to think about something.'

'What's that?' she whispered.

'Is Caldwell the man you want your son to emulate? Is he who you intend to hold up to Kyle as a role model?'

Long after he'd left, she stood in the middle of the room, unmoving, his words ringing in her ears. He was right. Leonard wasn't the proper role model for Kyle. Only one man could properly handle that responsibility. And that was Damien.

* * *

At the crack of dawn the next morning, Kyle crept into Sable's bedroom. Climbing on to her bed, he bounced on the mattress until, with a groan, she rolled over and fixed him with a fierce glare. 'What do you think you're doing, young man?' she demanded.

'Bouncin',' came the unconcerned retort.

She sighed. Clearly, her son was no easier to intimidate than his father. '*Why* are you bouncing on my bed at...' she fumbled for the clock '...six in the morning? Kyle!'

'Time to get up. Where's Day-man? I wants to play with him.'

She collapsed back against the pillows. Uh-oh. 'Stop bouncing. You're making me dizzy.'

He grinned, bouncing harder. 'Day-man! Day-man! Day-man!'

'He's not here.' But she wished he were, wished it with every fiber of her being. She released a soft groan, ruthlessly clamping down on the stray thought. She couldn't keep yearning for the impossible. She'd been down that road before and knew it led straight to disaster.

'When's he comin' back?'

'I'm not sure.' Hoping to end the inquisition, she grabbed him about the waist and tickled his ribs until he collapsed laughing. 'Come on, munchkin. Let's get breakfast.'

'Day-man comin'?' he asked, gazing expectantly up at her.

She sighed. 'No, Kyle. He's not coming for breakfast.'

To her disgust, the questions about Damien set the pattern for all of Saturday. Since business demands had taken up so much of her time these past two weeks and it was Millie's day off, Sable decided that a trip to the zoo would be a welcome treat.

'Can Day-man come?' Kyle instantly questioned.

'Not this time.' He didn't protest, but she could tell by the frown creasing his brow that her answer didn't please him. 'We'll invite him next time,' she offered, hoping it would suffice. To her relief, he accepted her suggestion without further complaint.

It was a perfect day, the weather warm and sunny, a light breeze alleviating the heat. She snapped a thousand pictures of Kyle imitating the various animals. And the whole time she thought about the situation with Damien. She'd been wrong not to tell him the truth last night. He wanted Kyle to be his son, she realized with a guilty pang. She'd seen the truth in his eyes, heard it in his voice. And, no matter what she'd said, he'd be a good father.

As for her accusation that he'd be unable to let down his guard enough, that he wouldn't risk his heart...Kyle would take care of that. Before Damien even knew what hit him, his son would slip in and take hold. It saddened her to think of all the years the two had already lost. She couldn't allow them to lose any more, not when it was within her power to prevent it. She couldn't be that selfish, couldn't allow her fears to stop her from doing what she knew to be right.

'Mommy,' Kyle shouted. 'I see Day-man!'

Before she could stop him, he took off, racing toward a man standing by the lion pit. His height and streaky brown hair resembled Damien's, but Sable realized instantly that Kyle had made a mistake. By the time she'd reached her son, he'd realized it too, and darted back to her side.

'I'm sorry,' she panted, breathless from her run. 'He thought you were someone else.'

'Hey, no harm done,' the man replied, offering an engaging grin.

Kyle clung to her legs, glaring at the stranger, furious that he wasn't Damien. 'Where's Day-man?' he demanded. 'I wants him here.'

She gathered him close, giving him a consoling hug and kiss. He returned her embrace with childish enthusiasm. How much longer would that last? she couldn't help but wonder. Soon he'd be too big, too embarrassed for such open affection. 'Damien promised he'd see you soon. And he will. You'll have to be patient.'

Kyle set his chin. 'T'morrow,' he insisted.

'We'll see. No promises, though.'

She handed him the camera and showed him how to snap a picture. The distraction worked...this time. But, knowing her son, it wouldn't last. He wouldn't be satisfied with anything less than Damien's presence. She closed her eyes, facing the inescapable facts. Kyle should have a strong male role model. Someone to share those special father-son activities. Someone to look up to and imitate. The time had come to surrender to the inevitable.

The time had come to tell Damien the truth about Kyle.

CHAPTER NINE

WITH her mind made up, Sable didn't dare wait until Monday to confront Damien with the truth. Instead she decided to track him down Sunday evening after dinner, her best chance of catching him at home. By delaying until then, she'd also have another day to spend with Kyle, and wouldn't have to leave him with Millie until after he'd been put down for the night.

She took full advantage of the few hours allotted her, the brief time she had with her son both precious and fleeting. And with every passing moment she realized how many special occasions Damien had missed . . . and how much he would resent her for that loss. Immediately after she'd tucked Kyle into bed, she left for Damien's. It had been years since she'd been this way—crossing the Golden Gate Bridge and driving into the hills above Sausalito.

It was like coming home.

She pulled into the driveway, parking at the side of the house as she'd done countless times before. A string of low-wattage outdoor lights marked the pathway to the house, and she climbed the steps along the terraced bank to the front door, dreading the moment she'd see Damien, dreading the conversation to come.

Lute answered her knock, greeting her with a smile of satisfaction. 'Ah. Miss Sable. I've been expecting you.'

She hesitated, gazing up in bewilderment. 'You have?'

'Most definitely.' He stepped back. 'Please come in. Damien is out right now, but you may wait for him, if you wish.'

'Thank you, I would.' She followed him into a huge common room that overlooked the water. 'How did you know I'd drop by?'

A slight smile touched his face. 'Your conscience would force you to. You would want to correct Mr Damien's assumption that your son was fathered by Leonard Caldwell.'

She stared at him, stunned. 'You *know*? How?'

'It was not an unreasonable conclusion, once I heard of young Kyle's existence.' He turned to face her. 'There were many mistakes made five years ago. Neglecting to tell Mr Damien you were pregnant was but one, am I right?'

'Yes,' she conceded. 'Though somehow I doubt Damien will be as tolerant as you over this particular mistake.'

He stroked his beard, his pale blue eyes filled with sympathy. 'Time is often needed to rectify these errors. And time is often essential to bring the situation full circle and allow for healing...for understanding. I think that is true in this case.'

He was right, of course. How he was able to see it so clearly escaped her, but he'd focused on the most critical elements. Five years ago Damien hadn't been ready to trust, hadn't been ready to hear the truth, let alone accept it. An apprehensive frown creased her brow. 'I just hope I haven't waited too long,' she murmured.

'Perhaps you have. Perhaps not.' He gave a small shrug. 'We shall see. I will bring you something to drink, and then I must leave you. Damien will return soon. Until he does, please make yourself comfortable.'

For a long time she stood by the window, darkness stealing into the room like a soft, protective blanket. She stared down at the lights of the town and harbor, and out across the wide, majestic sweep of the bay, with a calm she hadn't experienced in ages. A quarter moon slipped into the sky, its benevolent radiance a balm to her soul.

For the first time since Damien's return, she felt at peace. No matter what happened now, she'd finally confront a fear that had haunted her for five long years, face it and deal with it. She'd also correct a cruel wrong. Kyle would have a father and Damien would have a son. Nothing could be more important than that.

After what seemed an eternity, Damien's key scraped in the lock at the front door and she turned, waiting for him. Her heart pounded in her breast and her mouth grew dry. She gripped her hands together, praying for the strength to get through the coming discussion. He strode into the room, not bothering to switch on the lights, the moonlight apparently providing him with all the illumination he needed.

He unbuttoned his shirt and crossed to the small wet bar at the opposite end of the room to her. She heard the chink of glass as he poured a finger of whiskey, heard his almost inaudible sigh as he sipped the liquor. Moving toward her, he placed his glass on a side table and stripped off his shirt. He tossed it carelessly over the back of a chair and picked up his drink again, running a hand through the mat of hairs covering his chest.

He still hadn't seen her. She swallowed against the thickness in her throat. She should say something. But she didn't want to. She wanted to watch him—watch the animal grace of his movements, watch the ripple of muscles when he lifted the glass to his mouth, watch the play of light and shadow as moonlight danced across his bronzed chest and arms.

She knew the instant he sensed her presence. His entire body tensed and he pivoted with a swiftness that took her by surprise. 'Sable?' He spoke softly, his voice deep and husky, laced with irresistible demand.

'I should have said something when you first came in,' she hastened to tell him. 'I'm sorry, I——'

His glass hit the table beside him with a crash and words deserted her. She stared as he approached, her eyes huge and dark, and filled with a helpless vulnerability. He stopped inches from her. Silently, he reached for her, sliding his hand along the curve of her hip, drawing her close. She inhaled sharply, every sense keenly attuned to the bare expanse of his chest, the sultry warmth of his body, the unique, musky scent of him.

'I was just thinking about you... about us,' he said in a quiet undertone. 'You wanted to choose the time and place we made love.' He cupped her chin, tilting her head until the moonlight splashed across her face, revealing every fleeting nuance. 'Has the time come? Is this where and when, Sable? Is that why you're here?'

She shook her head. 'No. This has nothing to do with our agreement.'

His smile glimmered in the darkness. 'Good. Then it can be for the two of us. No conditions, no bargains, no deals. Just you and me. Together. The way it should be.'

'I haven't come to make love,' she started to tell him.

He lifted an eyebrow. 'Are you sure?' His hold tightened, and he tucked her into the cradle of his thighs, his eyes darkening at her small cry of distress. 'Are you positive?'

She fought the desire streaking through her, fought for sanity, fought for words and the breath to speak them. And all the while her hands crept up the ridged expanse of his abdomen, slipping into the thatch of crisp brown hair covering his chest. 'I came to talk.'

'No!' He objected with a vehemence that astonished her. 'No more talk. I'm sick of the arguments, of the suspicion. I want you, Sable. I want you without conditions, without questions, without doubts. Just you and me, a man and a woman, together the way nature meant us to be.'

'You make it sound so poetic,' she whispered sadly. 'But it's just lust, just sex . . . not love.'

He brushed her mouth with his thumb, the touch so gentle and tender that it made her want to weep. 'It was never just sex between us and it never will be.' But she noticed he didn't call it love either.

He didn't give her time to think, let alone argue. Without waiting for a response, he bent slightly and lifted her into his arms. She buried her face in the crook of his neck, pressing her lips to the warm juncture there, aware that her very silence committed her. She'd steal these few cherished moments for herself, give herself one last night to look back upon when all else had been irretrievably lost. It wasn't right and it wasn't fair, but it was as essential right now as the very air she breathed.

Once in the bedroom, he removed his arm from beneath her knees, allowing her to slip down the length of him. Her breasts grazed his chest and his breath quickened in response. The buttons of her blouse were a barrier swiftly dispensed with, the silk blouse stripped from her and sent floating to the floor. The thin, lacy bra provoked a more leisurely exploration. He traced the line between French silk and creamy skin, dipping into the cups to palm the softness within.

Sable moaned, the sound whispering between them. 'Damien, please.'

'Please what?' he demanded. 'Tell me what you want, my love.'

'I want you,' she confessed. 'I want you to make love to me—not out of revenge, but because you need me as much as I need you.'

He unclasped the tiny hooks at her back, the straps of her bra dropping from her shoulders, the silk falling away. 'This isn't revenge,' he told her, his eyes burning with a fierce heat. 'This is inevitable.'

She knew he was right, knew she belonged with him and only him, that they had been building toward this moment since he'd first reappeared in her life. He dropped to one knee, his hand cupping the back of her calf, before drifting upward beneath her skirt to the garters anchoring her stockings. With a flick of his thumb he released them one by one. She trembled within his hold, her fingers sinking into his hair as she fought for balance. Like the brush of a feather, the nylons glided down her legs. He lifted one foot, then the other, removing them.

And then he rose, his hand tugging at the zipper of her skirt, stripping away her remaining garments in one easy move. She stood before him, motionless, vulnerable and afraid, yet wanting his possession with a desperation she couldn't deny. Moonlight etched a path across the room, caressing her nudity, the silvery glow turning her skin to alabaster and sparkling in her hair like stars glittering in a midnight sky.

'So beautiful,' he murmured, molding her breast with his hand. 'So perfect.'

Tears gathered in her eyes and she bowed her head, pressing her lips to his chest. He groaned, the sound ripped from his throat, savage and raw. She felt the intensity of his desire and nervous dread feathered along her spine. 'It's been a long time,' she told him softly. 'I'm not sure I'm ready for this.'

'It's all right. There's no hurry,' came his gentle assurance. 'I won't hurt you.'

But he already had hurt her. And she knew, as surely as the sun would rise in the morning, that he would hurt her again. Worse, she would let him.

Once again he swept her into his arms. He was all strength, tough sinew and taut muscle and she reveled in his maleness. He carried her to the bed and placed her tenderly on the sheets. When at last he joined her, there was nothing between them—nothing but moist heat and sweet surrender. She reached for him, opening to him, soaring on wings of endless passion. And he took her, affording her that wondrous deliverance that she could find only in his arms, taking her body as completely as he had taken her heart. And as the night passed she fell in love all over again, helplessly, hopelessly, endlessly.

Forever.

Morning slipped silently into the room. For Sable, it came all too early. Sitting on the edge of the bed, Damien woke her, brushing the curls from her face, his fingers drifting across her cheek in a fleeting caress. She stirred, opening her eyes and blinking sleepily up at him.

'Good morning,' he said simply.

'Good morning, yourself,' she replied with a yawn, then looked at him in surprise. 'You're dressed for work.'

'I decided to go in early.' She started to throw back the sheet, but he stopped her, pressing her back against the pillows. 'You have plenty of time to get ready.'

She studied his expression nervously. Not a hint of passion marked his face. He returned her regard with a steady gaze, his green eyes cool and detached. This didn't look good. 'We need to discuss something before you leave,' she said, plucking at the bedcovers.

'Yes, I know.'

She didn't care for his tone and sat up, sweeping her hair from her eyes. 'I'm at a bit of a disadvantage here,' she murmured, tugging the sheet more fully across her breasts. 'Or was that the idea?'

He didn't answer her question, instead asking one of his own. 'Why did you come here last night? You said to talk. Talk about what?'

She took a deep breath. 'About Kyle,' she admitted.

He nodded, as though he'd known all along. 'I woke up in the middle of the night and couldn't get back to sleep because something was bothering me, teasing at the back of my mind. I started thinking about why you'd come, what could be so urgent. And then I thought about Kyle. All of a sudden the answer was there.' He looked at her, his eyes dark and turbulent. 'Kyle's my son, isn't he?'

The words hung between them, stark and divisive. 'Yes,' she whispered, and waited apprehensively for his response. It wasn't long in coming.

'My son.' Rage stirred, deep and powerful, sweeping across his face like a river in full flood. '*My son*! And you allowed Caldwell to get his hands on him. You gave that bastard my child! How could you do that?'

'I didn't *give* him anything,' she was swift to deny. 'I married him. He was Kyle's stepfather. There's a difference.'

He stood, moving away from her as though he couldn't bear to be too close. 'Don't split hairs with me. You allowed him to raise Kyle. You kept our child's existence a secret from me. Tell me why you did it,' he ordered. 'Explain it to me so I can understand.'

'You know how it ended between us.' She clutched the sheet in a white-knuckled grip. 'You refused my phone calls, wouldn't see me. You've never denied that——'

'That's an excuse!' His hands clenched, his chest rising and falling as though he'd run a marathon. 'You could have found a way to get in touch if it was that important. Hell, you knew where I lived, where I worked. It wouldn't have been that difficult to force a confrontation.'

She knelt on the bed, pulling at the sheet and wrapping it around her like a sarong. Lord, she'd give just about anything for some clothes. But she didn't dare take the time, didn't dare postpone this conversation for another second. 'You were out of the country by the time I realized I was pregnant. What was I supposed to do? Tramp through the jungles of South America until I found you? I had to put the welfare of my child first.'

'*Our* child,' he flashed back, his eyes dark with condemnation. 'And marrying Caldwell was not putting Kyle's welfare first. He was an easy way out. You couldn't have managed on your own, or gotten in touch with me when I returned? You had to sell yourself to that man?'

'I didn't sell myself to him!' She fought the urge to weep, refusing to betray any sign of weakness. Logic was all Damien would understand—cold, hard logic. She lifted her chin. 'What if I had gotten through to you? How would you have responded if I'd come to you claiming to be pregnant?'

He didn't answer immediately. At last he admitted, 'I'd have suspected you either made it up or——' He broke off, thrusting a hand through his hair.

'Or asked whose baby it was,' she finished for him. 'By the time I realized I was pregnant, I worked for Leonard. You'd already accused me of having an affair with him. Remember?'

'I remember.'

'This would have been all the proof you needed. You would never have believed you were the father. And even if you had, in your anger, you might have been tempted to use Kyle against me. I couldn't let you do that.' She bowed her head. 'It would have destroyed me.'

A muscle jerked in his cheek. 'So, why didn't you tell me about Kyle sooner?'

'When? After his birth?' She bit down on her lip, regret touching her features. 'I couldn't do that to Leonard. Not after all he'd done for me.'

Damien's mouth tightened. 'How about a year ago, when Leonard died? How about over two weeks ago, when I joined Caldwell's? Why the *hell* didn't you tell me then?'

She shook her head. 'I couldn't risk telling you the truth. Not when you were so intent on revenge.'

'And last night?' Cynicism edged his words. 'Tell me, Sable, what was that all about?'

She gazed at him in alarm. 'I don't understand.'

'Yes, you do. What was the point of last night? Did you hope going to bed with me would temper my reaction?'

'No! Don't you dare even suggest such a thing.'

He took a step closer. 'Or perhaps you were fulfilling our agreement, after all.'

She refused to back down, to show the slightest sign of intimidation. 'I keep telling you, there was no agreement. You demanded I sleep with you the same way you demanded I sell out to you. But in the end I would have refused. I won't go to bed with you just to satisfy your lust for revenge.'

'Then what was last night?' he repeated.

She looked at him, her heart breaking. 'I thought last night we made love,' she whispered. 'I guess I was wrong.'

He didn't contradict her. His eyes narrowed, his face growing taut and remote. 'I have to get to work,' was all he said, and turned from her. But he paused at the doorway, his back to her, throwing over his shoulder the words, 'You should have told me, Sable. I deserved that much.'

In another moment he'd leave, and she might never have another chance to explain her actions. 'I was afraid!' she cried, in her desperation admitting her deepest terror. 'I was afraid you might try and take Kyle away from me.'

'I still might,' he replied harshly, and walked away.

'You don't mean that! You can't mean that!' But it was too late. He was gone.

Sable didn't waste any time after that. She hurried to dress, desperate to get home, to get away. The house was silent and empty as she left, Lute nowhere to be seen. Climbing into her car, she headed back toward the city, the morning rush-hour traffic making the trip interminable. Once home, she showered and changed, painfully aware that her arrival at work would be delayed still another hour. Sure enough, by the time she walked through the front door at Caldwell's, it was well past nine.

'Good morning, Janine,' she greeted her secretary with a calm she didn't come close to feeling. 'How was your weekend?'

'Just fine, thank you.'

'Anything I should know about before we get started?' Sable asked, pausing by the door to her office.

Janine hesitated, her gaze slipping away. 'I...I'm not sure.'

Sable frowned. 'You're not sure?' What in the world did that mean? And then it hit her. Damien! She didn't know how, she didn't know why, but without a doubt he was behind that odd look on her secretary's face. 'What's going on?'

'It's just...' Janine shoved her glasses higher on the bridge of her nose, her pale blue eyes glinting behind the huge lenses. 'The board is meeting in the conference room, but they didn't say anything about you joining them. I——'

Sable didn't wait to hear more. Without another word, she hastened down the hallway toward the boardroom. Already she could hear muffled voices coming from behind the sturdy oak panel, voices raised in argument. She didn't bother to knock. She thrust open the door and walked right in.

Silence descended on the room with a stunning immediacy. They were all there, seated around the conference table, every one of them wearing identical expressions of outrage mingled with guilt. All except Damien. He sat at the end of the table, in her seat, clearly in charge, and as cool and commanding as she'd ever seen him.

She closed the door behind her with a decisive click. 'Am I interrupting something?' she asked in a deceptively calm voice.

'Sable! We...I... Damien...' Cornelius stuttered to a stop, ducking his head like a schoolboy caught cheating in an exam.

She folded her arms across her chest, eyeing the board members one by one. Only Damien could return her look. She fixed her attention on him. 'What's this about?' she demanded.

He leaned back in her chair. 'We're having a little talk about information leaked to Dreyfus Industry.'

'Leaked!' For a minute, Sable thought her legs would fold beneath her. 'You're joking.'

'I assure you, it's no joke.'

'But I thought Patricia——'

He shook his head. 'It would seem your guess about Patricia was wrong. She's not involved.'

She stared at the board members in bewilderment. 'Why wasn't I told about this? Why didn't you wait until I came in before starting?'

A wintry smile touched Damien's mouth. 'Because you're the prime suspect.'

Pain ripped through her, pain and anger and disbelief. So this was how he'd decided to take his revenge, to get even for Kyle. How could he? She closed her eyes, grief stealing over her. *How could he*? 'I won't let you do this,' she whispered. 'I didn't leak any information. It's not possible.'

'It came from you, my dear,' Cornelius spoke up at long last, his tone weary. 'Damien has incontrovertible proof.'

She opened her eyes. This wasn't the time to show weakness. She had to be strong, uncover the facts so that she could straighten this out. She stepped further into the room, her gaze never once leaving Damien. 'And what is this proof?'

He picked up the file in front of him and flipped it open. Removing a set of papers, he tossed them down the length of the table. They were the bid sheets she and Damien had worked on together for Dreyfus. 'The figures I gave you... they were false. I would have thought you'd have learned your lesson five years ago.'

She left the papers scattered across the table and lifted her chin. 'Oh, that's right. That's how you caught me last time, isn't it?'

'And you fell for it again.'

She gave a careless shrug. 'Just out of curiosity, how did you manage it?'

'I called the president of Dreyfus and warned him that a competitor may come calling with a copy of our bid— but that the figures would be wrong and to discredit it. He phoned and—surprise, surprise—a competitor had our prospectus in hand.'

'How did you know it came from me?' she questioned. 'Any number of people could have leaked it.'

'Each copy of our prospectus was coded.'

'Very clever, Damien,' she said, impressed. 'I assume my code showed up.'

He inclined his head in agreement. 'Yes. Your code showed up.'

'So, what do you intend to do?'

'What? No denials? Aren't you going to tell us you're innocent, that you've been set up again?'

'Would it do any good?'

'Sable! For heaven's sake,' Cornelius cried. 'Tell him you didn't do it. Explain to us what happened.'

She shook her head. 'There's no point,' she said gently. 'Damien would never believe me. Because that would mean he'd have to trust me, trust me despite all the evidence to the contrary. And he could never do that.'

To her astonishment, Damien smiled, genuine humor glittering in his eyes. 'No, I couldn't, could I?' Then his expression closed over and he turned his attention to the other board members. 'Gentlemen, it's time for a vote. All those in favor of removing Sable Caldwell as president and chairman of the board, say aye.'

There was a long moment of silence. Then, one by one, every last member murmured his assent.

'Any nays?'

No one said a word.

'Then the motion carries.'

For a split second, Sable didn't move, couldn't move. Then she stiffened her spine, glaring at each one of them in turn, her contempt plain to see. 'It would appear you've won after all, Damien. I'll tender my resignation, effective immediately.' Then, without another word, she left the room.

CHAPTER TEN

SABLE hastened back to her office, thrusting open the door and dragging air into her lungs in great, heaving gulps. How could he? How could Damien do that to her? Did he really believe in her guilt? Or was this part of a larger scheme—a more merciless form of revenge now that he knew about Kyle? What in heaven's name was she going to do?

'Mrs Caldwell?' Janine stepped from the shadows by the window. 'Are you all right?'

Sable started, lifting a hand to her throat. 'Janine! I...I didn't see you. I...' She closed her eyes, struggling for control. 'I'm fine, thank you.'

'Is there something I can do?'

'No,' she said, then changed her mind. 'Wait. Yes, there is. I wonder if you'd mind getting me a box from the mailroom?' she asked quietly.

'Is there something wrong?' Janine stepped closer. 'What's happened?'

Sable fought to keep her voice level, to keep from expressing the emotions that threatened to rip her apart. More than anything she wanted some privacy in which to break down and weep. 'I suppose you should know,' she said with a weary sigh. 'I've resigned. Effective immediately. If you could get a box for me, I can——'

'Resigned!' the secretary interrupted. 'Whatever for?'

'Janine, please.' Sable's voice broke and she covered her face with hands that trembled, struggling to pull herself together. 'There's been a leak within the company.

171

It's been traced to me, so I've been forced to resign,' she confessed.

'A leak?' Janine adjusted her glasses, her brows drawn together in a frown. 'You mean the information on one of our bids was given out to another construction company?'

'Yes.'

'But...why in the world would they think you did it?'

'I'd rather not go into that right now, if you don't mind,' Sable said, fast approaching the end of her rope. 'A box. I really need a box so I can pack my things.'

To her eternal relief, Janine obeyed without further comment. Sable glanced around the room, tears glittering in her eyes. So, it finally ended. First Leonard, then Patricia, and now, at last, she'd be gone too. And Damien would have won. He'd have exacted his revenge. Or would he have?

What about Kyle? she wondered uneasily.

'Mrs Caldwell?' Janine reentered the room. 'I have a box for you and some newspaper to wrap any breakables. Shall I help you pack your things?'

Sable nodded. 'Thank you. I'd appreciate that.'

It didn't take long. They removed the knickknacks from the credenza and from the top of her desk, and all the while Janine talked—talked endlessly, offering soothing little homilies interspersed with denigrating comments about Damien. Sable listened with only half an ear, tempted to defend him, but knowing she'd be wasting her time. Janine wouldn't change her mind about Damien—any more than Damien would change his about Sable's guilt.

She picked up Kyle's vase, running a finger over the bright primary colors. She'd known all along that

Damien was incapable of trusting. He hadn't believed her before, hadn't supported her; why would she expect him to this time? But what she hadn't anticipated was how badly that defection would hurt. She wrapped the vase in paper, facing one inescapable fact. She loved him. Loved him with all her heart. And somehow she couldn't quite accept that he could hold her in his arms, share such a passionately magical moment as last night, without feeling something in return. It just wasn't possible.

'I don't care what anyone says.' Janine continued her non-stop chatter. 'I'm sure if you leaked that information you had a good reason.'

'If I...' Sable looked at her secretary in shock, yanked from her thoughts with brutal suddenness. Where had that come from? 'Janine, I had nothing to do with that leak. How could you even think such a thing? Surely *you* know me better than that?'

Janine stirred uncomfortably. 'Of course I do, Mrs Caldwell. If you say you didn't do it, I believe you. It's just...'

Sable gazed at her secretary in despair. Would she be branded a thief forever, tainted in everyone's eyes by accusations that didn't have one iota of truth to them? 'It's just what?'

The secretary shrugged. 'I wanted you to know that I wouldn't blame you if you had leaked the information.'

'But I——' Sable broke off. What was the use? 'Thank you. I appreciate your support.'

If Janine noticed the irony in the comment, she gave no sign. She picked up the photo of Leonard, staring at it for a long moment. 'Losing that account to A.J. Construction would put Mr Hawke in a very bad light,' she said, almost contemplatively. 'After what he did to

Leonard, to Miss Patricia … it would be the perfect revenge—a well-deserved revenge. I just thought you
should know…I don't blame you.' She placed the photo
gently into the box and closed the flaps.

'Am I interrupting?' Damien stood at the door, his
gaze sweeping over them with nerve-racking intensity.

'What is it, Damien?' Sable asked with a weary sigh.
She gestured toward the box. 'As you can see, we're
almost done here. What more could you possibly want?'

He looked at Janine and jerked his head toward the
door. She didn't need any further urging. She slipped
from the room, leaving Sable to face Damien alone. He
slammed the door closed. 'We have to talk.'

'Talk about what?' she demanded. She didn't want to
talk. She wanted to be held by him, kissed by him, told
that he loved her and believed in her. Clearly, she wanted
the impossible. 'Shall we discuss how you stole my
company out from under me? Or how you framed me
for something I didn't do? Or shall we examine your
quest for revenge—revenge because I married Leonard,
because I didn't tell you about Kyle?'

'I'm not here to debate our personal life.'

She folded her arms across her chest. 'Oh, that's right,
this is strictly business, isn't it? I shouldn't take it per-
sonally. Well, how about this…? Now that I'm gone
there won't be anyone left to blame when we lose another
big account. You're so busy pointing the finger at me
that you're neglecting to put your energies where they're
truly needed—into finding the guilty party.'

A grim smile tugged at his mouth. 'I think by removing you from the scene the leaks will stop.'

'Well, you're wrong.' Hopelessness glimmered in her
dark eyes. 'Why didn't you come to me? Why didn't

you discuss the Dreyfus situation with me so we could work together to find whoever leaked the information?'

He shrugged. 'Since the prospectus was yours, it seemed ... ill-advised to discuss it with you.'

'So instead you just oust me from the board based on the evidence from the prospectus alone?' It didn't make sense. She didn't know why, but she suspected he was being evasive. 'How long have you known about our bid being leaked to Dreyfus?'

He hesitated, then admitted, 'Their CEO called me on Saturday.'

She turned white. '*Saturday*!'

'We met Sunday afternoon to hammer out a private agreement. That's why I was so late returning home.'

'Which means...' She stared at him in despair. 'When I came to see you last night, you knew it was my prospectus that had been used. *You knew*! And yet you still made love to me, led me to believe ...' It was a struggle to speak, to say the words without breaking down. 'When I came to you last night, you'd already planned to remove me from the board, hadn't you?'

'Yes.' The word hung between them, bald and cold and inescapable.

'How could you?' she whispered. 'How could you do such a thing?'

His eyes narrowed, turning hard and distant. 'You're always talking about trust. I should trust you, support you, believe in you despite all evidence to the contrary. Where's your trust, Sable?' He approached, catching her arm and yanking her close. She tried to fight, to pull away, but he wouldn't release her. He cupped her face, his thumb feathering across her cheek. 'It's different when the shoe's on the other foot, isn't it? Blind trust. You expect it, but you're unwilling to give it. The moment there's so much as a whisper of a doubt, you suspect the worst.'

'And why not?' she cried, catching his shirt in her fists. She glared up at him, wishing she could look into those cool, remote features without wanting him. Wishing she didn't care so very, very much. Wishing something as simple as his touching her cheek wouldn't stir such a passionate response. 'What have you ever done to make me believe in you, trust in you? You've come into my life again, demanding I sell out to you, demanding I sleep with you——'

'What about Kyle?' he came right back at her. 'What about Leonard? What about all the secrets you've kept from me? It's a two-way street, Sable. You want trust, but you aren't willing to give it any more than I am.'

'It's never been a two-way street with you,' she instantly denied. Her hands slipped from his chest and she took a small step away from him. 'You've never been willing to let me in, not completely. Isn't it time you told me why?'

His hand fell from her face and he let her go, his mouth tightening. For a minute, she didn't think he'd answer. Then he said, 'It's an old story. Over long ago.'

'But it changed you,' she replied. 'It has to do with that night in the bar, doesn't it? When you were nineteen and Lute saved your life.'

He nodded. 'I was a fool. I thought my world had ended.'

'Why?' she whispered. 'Tell me why.'

He ran a hand across the back of his neck, staring at the carpet, lost in thought. Finally, he spoke. 'I came from a wealthy background. Big house, fancy cars, top schools. And then one day I woke up and it was all gone. My father's business went under and he declared bankruptcy. It was…difficult, but we knew we'd work it out, that we'd recover.'

'Then why…?'

'I had a girlfriend. We were both in our second year at Stanford University. It was serious—we talked about a future, marriage. In my youthful arrogance I was certain she'd stand by me, that my family's financial reversal wouldn't matter.'

Compassion touched her. 'But it did.'

He inclined his head. 'Once knowledge of the bankruptcy became public, I wasn't even allowed in the door. I got it into my head that it was her parents keeping us apart, that we were some sort of modern-day Romeo and Juliet. So I slipped into her room that night only to discover that Jennifer felt the same way her parents did. I was welcome to come in the back door, she graciously offered; she'd even be happy to let me in her bed again. But marriage? An open relationship? Not a chance.'

Her heart went out to him. 'And so you learned that women were only after one thing.'

He didn't deny it. 'Money is a great motivator,' he said in a dry voice.

'It can be.' She approached, laying her hand on his arm. 'But love is an ever greater one. Jennifer didn't love you or she would have stood by you. She betrayed you.' Sable waited for that to sink it, before adding, 'I never did.'

'Didn't you?' Weary cynicism tainted the question. 'Why should I believe that? Because you once claimed to love me?'

She didn't hesitate for a moment, didn't dare hesitate or evade the truth. 'Yes, Damien. I loved you five years ago and I love you now. I've always loved you. Do you really think last night would ever have happened if I didn't?'

His expression closed over. 'Why not? Or are you trying to tell me you also loved Caldwell?'

She refused to back down. Instead she looked him straight in the eye. 'I never made love to Leonard. Not once. Our marriage was strictly platonic. You're the only man I've ever made love to, the only man I've ever wanted to make love to.'

A muscle jerked in his jaw. 'Is this another lie?' He rasped out the question.

She shook her head. 'I've never lied to you—except about Kyle. And that was by omission only.'

'It was one hell of an omission!' His anger died as quickly as it had flared and he shot her a searching look. 'You're serious about your relationship with Caldwell?' At her nod, he asked, 'That last night we were together. Do you remember it?'

How could she forget? It had been the last time she'd seen him. They'd held each other through the night, making love with an ardor and desperation that she had never forgotten, knowing that their world was slowly being ripped apart by lies and suspicions. In the morning, he'd walked out her door and out of her life, refusing ever to see or speak to her again. 'I remember all too well.'

'I went to see Caldwell that day, to demand an explanation for the business we'd lost to them. He confirmed what you said—that you'd let certain information slip to Patricia without realizing who she was. He also said that once you did know, once the truth came out, you'd gone in with them, deciding to take your chances with Caldwell's. He claimed you'd leaked that last project on purpose and showed me a copy of our bid as proof.' He looked at her, his hands clenched, his body tensed as though for a blow. 'He also implied that you two were having an affair.'

'And you believed him,' she stated sadly. Oh, Leonard! Why did you do it? she lamented silently. Had she misjudged him all these years, seen him as her savior when in fact he'd been anything but?

Damien nodded. 'The evidence weighed heavily against you.' He released his breath in a long sigh. 'I don't know. It was...easier to buy his version.'

'I can only guess that Patricia managed to obtain that bid through ulterior means. I never knowingly gave the information to Caldwell's. But I was their unwitting conduit. I've never denied that.' She bit down on her lip. 'Do you still believe he told you the truth about me...about our relationship?'

'No.' Not a shred of doubt shaded his voice, and for the first time hope crept into her heart. 'There's something else you should know. I didn't blackball you with the other construction companies.'

She caught her breath. 'Leonard?'

'Leonard,' he confirmed. 'I suspect he did it so you'd have no other choice but to work for him. Your pregnancy must have played right into his hands.'

Had it happened that way? Was it possible? Later, when she had the time and privacy to consider what she'd learned, she could regret all that had happened five years ago. But more important matters concerned her now, more pressing problems. 'What about now, Damien?' she asked anxiously. 'What about the Dreyfus leak? What's going to happen?'

It was as though a door slammed in her face. His expression closed over and he shrugged. 'I'm looking into it,' he claimed.

'That's not what I mean.' She looked at him, confronting her worst fear. 'Are you going to prosecute?'

His gaze flashed to hers, an odd expression sweeping across his face. 'That's up to the board.'

She made an impatient gesture. 'You know the board will do whatever you recommend.'

'A decision hasn't been reached yet,' he insisted, refusing to give her the reassurance she so desperately needed.

So that was it. Despite all the grand words, despite all attempts to clear up their differences, nothing had changed. The tiny spark of hope she'd so carefully nurtured died. She cleared her throat. 'In that case, I want you to do something for me.'

'What is it?'

'If the board chooses to prosecute, I want you to take care of Kyle for me.'

He couldn't conceal his exasperation. 'What the hell are you talking about?'

'I'm talking about Kyle and what would be best for him,' she said carefully. 'I...I put it in my will years ago. If something happens to me, Kyle is to go to you. But I hadn't anticipated an eventuality like this. I hadn't thought about the possibility of...' She lifted her chin. 'You're to take him if things get nasty.'

She turned, unable to bear another minute. Snatching up her box of personal possessions, she fled from the room, hurrying down the hallway toward the elevators. Balancing the carton on her knee, she stabbed at the button. Finally the doors opened and she stepped into the car along with half a dozen others. Damien appeared then, sprinting between the doors at the last possible instant.

'We need to talk,' he announced, taking the box forcibly from her arms.

She refused to look at him, afraid he'd see the tears she was struggling to hold at bay. 'About what?' she asked softly, darting a quick glance at the other occupants. Why here? Why now? She couldn't take much more of this.

Damien didn't seem to care whether they had an audience or not. 'You'd trust me to take care of him?' he demanded. 'You'd trust me with Kyle?'

'I'd trust you with my life,' she declared passionately. 'Haven't you realized that yet? I'd trust you with my greatest possession—and that's Kyle. And if you say you don't believe me, or ask for proof, I'll never, ever forgive you.'

A youthful-looking executive turned to Damien. 'I believe her,' he offered. He glanced at Sable. 'I believe you.'

A shaky smile trembled on her lips. 'Thank you,' she murmured, blinking rapidly to clear the sudden tears. 'I appreciate that.'

Damien swore beneath his breath. 'Sable...I know you didn't do it.'

It took a full minute for his comment to sink in. The elevator stopped and a few of the passengers got off. The young executive started to, then changed his mind, staying put. The door closed again. 'What did you say?' she demanded.

'He said——'

She rounded on the eavesdropper. 'I heard what he said!' She peeked up at Damien, that tiny kernel of hope bursting to life once more. 'Say it again.'

A reluctant smile touched his mouth. 'I said, I know you didn't give our prospectus to Dreyfus.'

The elevator arrived at the ground floor and neither of them moved. 'Come back upstairs,' Damien said— softly, gently, tenderly. He glanced at the avidly watching executive and pointed at the open door. 'You. Off.'

An instant later they were alone and the elevator doors closed. It was like that first day when he'd approached her, only this time Damien hadn't come to de- stroy... but to heal. It wasn't until they were moving upward again that Sable gathered the nerve to ask the question uppermost in her mind. 'How do you know I'm not responsible? Do you have proof?'

'No. Yes.' He ran a hand through his hair. 'I don't have anything concrete, but...' He seemed to grapple with his response, searching for the right words. 'I've watched you, Sable. All the years we were together, you never demanded anything of me, and you gave every- thing. Then it went bad, and you fell in with Caldwell. But you stuck by him, too. As he lost one company after another, as his wealth diminished, you didn't walk away. Instead you rolled up your sleeves and pitched in to help. That shocked the hell out of me.'

'He was my husband.' There was no getting around that fact.

Damien shook his head. 'No, he wasn't. Not in any way that counted.'

'You still haven't explained why you decided I was innocent.'

'You said something to me once. You said that I should have known you could never betray me. That I should have moved heaven and earth to help prove your innocence.'

'What I said was that if you *loved* me you'd know I could never betray you. If you *loved* me, you'd move heaven and earth to prove my innocence,' she corrected him softly. 'So... do you? Do you love me?'

His eyes gleamed like polished jade. 'Why else would I have had you thrown off the board?'

The doors opened then, and the moment was lost before she could grab hold of it. He stepped from the car, and she followed, struggling to hide her disappointment. 'Why *did* you have me removed from the board?' she questioned as they headed back down the hallway.

He waited until they were in her office, with the door shut against all possible intruders. 'It's obvious someone hopes to pin this on you. I wanted you clear of the line of fire while I figured out who it was.'

'And have you?'

He shook his head, his frustration evident in the tense set of his shoulders and taut line of his mouth. 'No. Not yet.'

'Won't Alex Johnson tell you?' A small line formed between her eyebrows. 'I must admit, I don't understand it. I thought he wanted to avoid antagonizing you. So why in the world would he risk your anger again by——?'

'What did you say?' He tossed the box on her desk, heedless of any damage he might cause the contents. Turning to face her, he grabbed her by the shoulders. 'How did you know that?'

She stared at him in bewilderment. 'Know what?'

'How did you know it was Alex who approached Dreyfus? I never released that information. The only other person who could know is the thief.'

She stared at him, her eyes huge with anguish. No! It couldn't be happening. He'd just started to trust her again. He couldn't be accusing her of this. Not again.

She swayed, clutching at the lapels of his jacket. She couldn't continue living like this, spending a lifetime on the edge, constantly being doubted by him. She couldn't! If that was what he intended, there was no hope, no possibility of a future together.

'What are you asking me?' she whispered.

'Who told you it was Alex?' Damien demanded impatiently, sweeping a lock of hair from her face. 'Come on, Sable. Don't hold back now. Because whoever told you is the one we're looking for.'

For a long moment she couldn't speak, she was so overcome with emotion. He didn't doubt her. Dear God, he didn't doubt her! To her disgust, she burst into helpless tears. Throwing her arms around his neck, she lifted her tear-stained face to his. 'Please kiss me,' she begged. 'Quickly.'

He didn't need a second prompting. His mouth found hers, tasting, teasing, seducing with hot, desperate kisses. The rapture was instantaneous, raw and primitive, touching a primal chord deep in her soul. She couldn't seem to get enough, his touch healing the pain, driving away the suffering of the past few weeks... of the past few years. How long it was before the embrace ended she never knew.

He gazed down at her, brushing the dampness from her cheeks, his eyes dark with passion. 'Now will you tell me? Or do I need to use force?' he asked, his voice filled with tenderness. 'I can torture you with kisses, tie you to my bed for a month until you confess who told you about Alex.'

'As tempting as that sounds, I'll tell you.' She sighed. 'It was Janine.'

He nodded, not particularly surprised. 'Janine. I should have known.' A cold, ruthless light entered his eyes. 'Ask your secretary to step in here, will you?'

The next half hour was the most painful of Sable's life. It didn't take long for Damien to goad the truth from Janine. And, once the virulent outpour began, it flowed swift and deadly.

'Leonard never loved you,' she informed Sable venomously. 'He was using you. It was me he should have married...would have married. But Patricia convinced him not to. She told him the only way they could defeat Hawke Enterprises was if Leonard married you. It was the biggest mistake he ever made. Because of you he lost everything—his company, his health, even his life. But I wasn't about to let him die in vain. I got even.' She glared in triumph. 'No one suspected me or limited my access. After all, I've been with the company forever. So, I took you all on. First Patricia and then the two of you.'

Overwhelmed by Janine's malice, Sable slipped closer to Damien, burying her face against his shoulder. He didn't wait to hear any more. Calling for Security, he had Janine removed from the premises.

'What are you going to do to her?' Sable murmured, safe within the circle of his arms and determined not to leave his protective embrace anytime soon.

'I'm not sure. I'm reluctant to prosecute, but I also can't stomach the idea of her getting away with it. I expect we'll settle out of court.'

'She must have loved Leonard very much.'

Damien shook his head. 'That wasn't love, at least not the kind I'm familiar with.'

Sable licked her lips, staring up at him with her heart in her eyes. 'And what sort are you familiar with?' she whispered.

'The sort that withstands all adversity. The sort that never dies,' he responded promptly. His hand slid up her spine, molding her against his heat, stoking the fires that raged between them with such spontaneous abandon. His voice deepened. 'All I have to do is look at you, touch you, hear you speak and I realize how very much I love you.'

'But you came back for revenge,' she dared to remind him.

'That's what I told myself.' His fingers slipped into her hair and he brushed his mouth over hers, an infinitely gentle touch. 'But the truth is...I couldn't stay away. Why did you think I was so desperate to have you back in my bed? I knew once I had you there you'd be there to stay.'

And she would. 'What about the board? What are you going to tell them?'

A slow smile crept across his mouth. 'I'm going to demand to know why they had my wife removed as president and chairman of the board. And I'm going to tell them that if they ever do it again I'll get rid of every last one of them.'

She stilled. 'Your wife?'

The laughter died from his expression and he gazed down at her with stark intensity. 'If you'll have me. And if Kyle will have me.'

The tears came again, tears of sheer joy. 'I think I can convince him.'

'And you? Will you have me, Sable? Will you marry me?'

'Oh, yes. I love you, Damien. I can't imagine life without you. I don't want to imagine a life without you.'

There was no further need for words. His mouth came down to meet hers and she melted against him. It was finally over. The secrets of the past were laid to rest, and the future lay ahead, bright and beautiful and infinitely precious.

A future she intended to grasp with both hands and never let slip through her fingers again.